MW01132744

Other Books by Robert Eisenhart

Occabot

Investigator

Maenads

Manly

THE SPOKEN WORD

by

Robert Eisenhart

This book is a work of fiction. Names, characters, places,
brands, media, and incidents either are the product of the
author's imagination or are used fictitiously, and any resemblance
to actual persons, living or dead, events, or locales is entirely
coincidental. The author acknowledges the trademarked status
and trademark owners of various products referenced in this
work of fiction, which have been used without permission. The
publication/use of these trademarks is not authorized, associated
with, or sponsored by the trademark owners.

~~~

Chapter 1

Americans are certainly great hero-worshipers, and always take their heroes from the criminal classes.

—*Oscar Wilde*

The city had finally made good on the promise to install the anti-crime lights in *the projects*.

A white chalky glare outlined shadows in the night—stark as sidewalk tracings of homicide victims. However, this particular collection of shadows didn't view themselves as victims. And they did not appreciate the exposure.

People living in the buildings adjacent to the playground would come home off the night shift, or maybe they couldn't sleep so they'd sit up looking out their windows. They'd get to see drug buys go down, small stakes craps games between parked cars, and occasional acts of violence. With these new lights they could even see into the playground, to the bombed-out casualties of summer boredom. Those who walked, stumbled; those who sat, nodded. There was some good 'shit' on the street. Everyone was high.

It hadn't cooled down very much since the afternoon, but at

1

least it wasn't so goddamn sticky. Freddy 'D' thought it a fine fucking night, except for one thing—those fucking lights. They made everyone feel real uncomfortable, put upon. It was a direct assault upon their privacy. The whole place was lit up like a night game at Shea Stadium. Way too conspicuous! And the bugs! Goddamn lights attracted bugs.

Sitting on a park bench, Freddy D moved his rubbery hand in slow motion to scratch the mosquito bite on his face. "Fuck, this sucks, getting eaten alive out here!" He liked his *fuck* word; barely a sentence got by him without one.

His blank stare fixed on the park house. It had the look of a bunker. Some of the boys had broken into the bathroom again. They were getting high in there. Lately, the park men had to repair the lock almost daily.

The park men knew Freddy. Everyone knew Freddy. When he would see them, during the day, he would nod at them and they would concede a wary nod back. They seemed like okay guys. But they were 9-to-5'ers and they were up against full-time round-the-clock fuck-ups. Still you had to hand it to them, they were persistent. First they replaced the lock. Then they installed a metal plate around it. Then came a metal doorframe—the old wooden one had been whittled to shreds.

On this particular night the entire door stood removed from its hinges and leaning against the brick wall of the park house cubicle.

Alongside the building, under the heavy wire mesh that covered the windows, Willy Freeman balanced on his bike. His hazel eyes peered out from under a dusty head of thick brown hair that was overdue at the barber's. He looked up and down the walk. He was the lookout for the older guys, the guys inside. Most of them were in their twenties. But sometimes they let Willy hang out with them, even though he was only fifteen. Fifteen wasn't that young.

Willy had a nickname that had stuck with him from when he was a kid. Everyone called him *Spokes*. He used to always clip playing cards to the spokes of his bicycle so you could hear him coming—the *Evel Knievel* of the bicycle set. Word had it that he once rode around the entire projects doing a wheelie. To the twelve year olds that was hot shit. But what did they know; they were twelve.

Now he hung out with the big guys. He liked the way that made him feel. And they always let him bum cigarettes. Not that he was a heavy smoker, not really. He did it to look tough. Most of the big guys smoked Marlboros; some Kools. He smoked O.P. cigarettes—Other People's.

Still, they all liked Spokes. And just lately he'd become somewhat of a hero. It was 'cause of what happened a couple nights back. Spokes put *Goofball* Greg on his bike and managed to get the old junkie out of the playground before the cops got there. As usual, Greg's friends had left him. He was in no condition to run; he would've definitely been picked up if not for Spokes. Word got out about what Spokes had done and he was riding high. All the hopheads knew—on another night it might not be Greg.

3

Spokes could hear someone puke in the park house. It smelled bad in there—piss and smoke and puke. But there was a sink inside, running water to cook the *smack*. And it was convenient. Score at the park, get off in the park house—the busiest shooting gallery around.

The water fountain on the outside of the park house got turned off at night. That didn't make any fuckin' sense. Fuck the park men if their door gets broken.

Freddy D looked up as a city bus went flying by. This time of night there were only a handful of passengers on board. The end of the line was just around the corner; the driver was pushing it, slowing just enough to negotiate the turn.

A square-shouldered figure hung on the back of the bus. Pointy Puerto Rican cockroach killers found toeholds on the vents in the rear panel; his left arm hugged the side, fingers easily holding firm to the window frame. In his right hand he carried a giant boom box. A funky electric guitar riff came hard-driving straight for the projects, hijacking all ears for a quarter mile in all directions.

The guys on the corner caught sight of the sound and a straggly chorus of hoots and hollers went up, welcoming the wayward warrior. Wolfee was back in the neighborhood.

Before the bus coughed back up to speed, it deposited its nonpaying passenger. With taps on his shoes he jumped off and clicked his way into the park. There were several groups of guys clustered every few feet. He stopped at each to slap hands and exchange crude greetings.

Wolfee wasn't from the neighborhood. He came from a section of Brooklyn called East New York. But lately he had adopted the projects. That went both ways. As nuts as he was, he fit right in. Wolfee had a reputation that he had cultivated all over Brooklyn. It was generally accepted that he was "criminally insane." The boy liked to fight. He was always looking for "action." And at this place in time, the project park was "happening." A steady stream of cars pulled up to buy shit. But it wasn't the drugs that drew Wolfee. It was what went with them. Somehow he could sense being downwind from trouble. Not one of them blues singers, trouble following him wherever he goes; with Wolfee, it worked the other way 'round.

This time he had a plan. Along with his best friend, Freddy D, he was ready for a piece of the action....

Freddy D wasn't seeing too clearly but he recognized the walk, the ghetto blaster.

"Hey, Wolfee, over here!"

The newcomer cut away from the group at the park's entrance and walked over. There was the slap of a 'high five'. Wolfee sat down.

"Bro, word has it you movin' some good shit?"

Wolfee was white but where he lived it was all black. He talked and walked like a *brother*. Claimed the blacks called him *Maku*. Said it meant *White Devil*. He was the only white walking around Brownsville as he pleases. Said they leave him alone 'cause he's certifiably crazy. He was probably telling the truth.

"I got some boys down in Canarsie wanna buy all you got. I

told you this was gonna happen. With all the people I know..."

"Forget it, Wolfee. It's no fuckin' good."

"What do you mean 'It's no fuckin' good'? I know *good* when I see it. And that was some good shit, Bro."

"That's fuckin' not what I mean. I mean I sold the last of it."

"Well... get some more. I'm talkin' about a motherfuckin' franchise.... Where'd that shit come from, anyhow?"

"Rosey."

"He finally came through... It was about time.... Well, now we can get started... like we spoke about. You gotta get some more." Wolfee was all wound up. "We're gonna be big. With all the people I know... you're gonna be the biggest street dealer in Brooklyn. ...And I'll be your bodyguard. Nobody'll fuck wit my man, Freddy D."

If Wolfee wasn't so busy daydreaming out loud, he would've noticed that Freddy wasn't exactly sharing his enthusiasm. Freddy mumbled, "I can't fuckin' get no more shit"—Wolfee kept right on talking—"I got no fuckin' money."

He heard that. "Whadaya mean, you got no fuckin' money? You just sold a ton a' shit.... Where's the money?"

"It ain't *my* money. It wasn't *my* shit. I'm still fuckin' waiting for *my* shit. Rosey says he don't have it. This was somethin' different. Some guy fronted it to him... and I was just movin' it for him. It was like a favor. I got some for my fuckin' head, but that was all."

"You shittin' me...! And you gonna give him the money. Don't be an asshole. That *is* your money. He was supposed to get you shit, right! And you never got it. So that shit was your shit. Simple as that."

"Yeah, but he says he lost *my* money—some fuckin' whore ripped him off. Says he fell asleep in a hotel in the city and when he woke up... it was gone. He's real fuckin' sorry. Says he'll get my money for me as soon as he can. Either that... or the shit he was supposed to get me in the first fuckin' place. Meanwhile he's givin' me a dime for every five dimes I unloaded. It's a separate thing."

"If I were you I'd keep the money. Man, it's your money. That's all there is to it. He's fuckin' you and you keep bending over. Keep the fuckin' money." In a way Wolfee felt like he was the one getting ripped off. He had a lot riding on this deal. "I don't care how big a *rep* Rosey's got. You don't go around rippin' off guys from the neighborhood. It ain't right. We don't stand for that around here."

"You know what you're fuckin' saying, Wolfee. You're talkin' about Rosey. You want I should tell him he don't get his money?"

"It ain't *his* money, man. It's your money. You stole it. That makes it yours. I'll back you. I don't care who the fuck he is. You're my main man. Nobody fucks wit you. If they do, they fuck wit me. And you mess wit da Wolfee, you messin' wit one bad motherfucker."

"Gee, I don't know, Wolfee."

The high pitched buzz of a mosquito burrowed right into Wolfee's ear. He batted his head with an open palm and shook

7

his head violently. "Fuckin' mosquito!"

"It's them fuckin' lights brings all these fuckin' bugs."

They were talking real loud and Spokes could hear their conversation from where he was. He knew all about what was going down between Rosey and Freddy D. The whole park knew. Freddy D had robbed a house. He took the money he made and gave it to Rosey, who was supposed to get him some weight, to deal. It looked like Freddy had been ripped off.

Spokes peddled backwoods as he sat upon his trusty steed, the chain clicking. He pushed off from the wall, jerked up on the handlebars, and lifted into a spin. He stood on his right rear axle peg, propelling into a tight arc. As the momentum lifted the front tire higher off the ground, he kicked at the rear tire with his left foot—spinning himself in circles. From atop the twister he scoped three-sixty, checking the paths on both sides of the park house.

Rosey was entering the park.

Spokes dropped sudden-like. Then—dialing back on the excitement he was feeling—he rode nonchalantly past Freddy and Wolfee.

And he just happened to mention, "Hey, Freddy... Rosey's coming."

Having done that, he rode once around the park house and settled himself back against the wall, to wait. His adolescent face, an open book: *There's gonna be a fight!*

Freddy D and Wolfee didn't say another word to each other; their eyes were having a salient discussion.

It was interrupted by a voice. "Freddy." Rosey stood a few feet away. He was looking down at the ground. His eyebrows rose up in a twitch-like movement and he spit between his teeth. "Come 'ere." And it was as if the voice reached out and grabbed Freddy by the collar.

Freddy came forward, his head kept turned toward Wolfee until the last possible second when he was standing right in front of Rosey. He needed a last assurance. He wasn't going to be alone in this.

But Wolfee had suddenly grown standoffish.

Freddy took out a roll of bills, handed it over.

"I sold it all, no problem. People keep asking me if I can get more." Remarkable—two sentences without a single *fuck*.

Rosey turned his attention to counting the money.

"Hey, Rosey, what about *my* shit? If you can't get it, when do I get my money back?"

Rosey finished counting, then folded the money and pushed it into the tight front pocket of his pants.

"Listen, Freddy," he sounded annoyed, "I'm going to get you your money back. This money..." he tapped his pocket, "...isn't mine. I got to give this money to another guy who I owe for a lot longer time than I owe you. But I'm going to get your money, you understand...? I don't know when but you'll get it."

"Well... maybe that's not good enough."

"*What* did you say?"

Could Rosey have actually not heard? To Freddy it felt like he'd shouted. It had taken so much energy to muster the resolve.

9

Now he had to do it all over. So again—with somewhat less vehemence—he said, "Well... maybe that's not good enough."

Rosey started to squint, like maybe he wasn't seeing right either. What the hell kind of a look was that? Freddy couldn't tell. Was he hurt that he might not be trusted? Was he upset with himself? or pissed at Freddy? Maybe he was really sorry that he didn't have Freddy's money? or maybe he was disgusted that he, Eddy Rosen, was being talked to like that? It was a strange look. Then came the trademark raise of the eyebrows and squirt of spit between the teeth. "Freddy, I can't give you what I don't have, you understand? I'll try to get your money for you in a couple a' weeks."

"You said that a couple a' weeks ago. And now it's a couple a' weeks and I want my money." Now Freddy really was raising his voice and his hand motioned toward Rosey's pocket.

"I told you, this ain't my money. You're not the only person I owe."

"I know you think there's nothing I can do about it, but you're wrong. I can fuckin' do something about it. You don't think so, but I—"

Freddy was turning his head as he spoke, shooting a glance toward Wolfee. That was a mistake. He should've never taken his eyes off Rosey's hands. The right hand smashed into the side of his head with a force there was no standing up to. Freddy D's whole body slapped the ground. Rosey stood over him.

Both fists still clenched, Rosey looked to Wolfee. "And you, Doggie, you got a problem, too?"

Wolfee was muttering and sputtering, looking down at the ground, looking at Freddy who was trying to lift himself up but fell back down utterly destroyed.

"What did you say?" Cords stood out on Rosey's forearms, his feet planted squarely.

"No problem."

"That's what I thought you said."

Spokes couldn't believe his eyes. Rosey had put Freddy D away with one shot. And Freddy was supposed to be a pretty tough guy.

Rosey reached out and helped him up. "Hey, Freddy, I'm sorry I had to do that, but you made me. You say you can do something about it—okay, do it." Rosey held onto Freddy's left arm. He knew Freddy was a lefty. Rosey was a cautious man. Overly cautious in this instance. Freddy needed the grip to be steadied. It was over, but Rosey was going to play it for all it was worth. He shook Freddy and went on. "I ain't got your money. I *was* going to try to get you your money. I told you. But if you're going to be like this, you can go fuck yourself, you understand?"

Rosey did his twitch and spit, then he let go and walked away toward the park house.

As he passed Spokes he showed just a trace of a smile. He held out his hand hip-high palm down and snapped his fingers. "Hiya, Spokes."

"Hiya, Rosey…. Got a cigarette?"

He stopped and gave Spokes a Marlboro, then went into the men's room.

Spokes couldn't have been more honored. That was Rosey, the toughest guy in the projects, and he talked to Spokes like they were buddies.

Wolfee took hold of Freddy, sat him back down on the bench. He tried to explain. He wasn't going to let Rosey get away with this. It was just that now wasn't the time, but he—

Freddy didn't want to hear it. He pushed himself up and went stumbling past Spokes. His eyes, a void. The fear of confronting Rosey had momentarily caused him to get straight. Now that it was over, he reverted back to his stoned self. He was heading for the water fountain, intending to splash some water on the dull hot sensation of pain coming from the side of his head. He got right up to it before he realized it wasn't working. There was the sink in the men's room, but he wasn't going in there. He cursed, "Fuckin' fountain don't work. My fuckin' head aches. Fuckin' mosquitoes are eating me alive. And these fuckin' lights are driving me crazy. It's like a fuckin' interrogation, bright light shining in my eyes all the fuckin' time. I can't take it. This whole fuckin' place sucks."

He went and sat back down by Wolfee. Neither one would raise his eyes to look at the other. This went on for several interminable moments.

Then, Wolfee—rising to his feet like he was rising to the occasion—declared, "It's those fuckin' lights.... You're right, Freddy. This park used to be an out-a'-sight place to hang before those... fuckin' lights. I'll be back.... You stay put. I'll be right back."

Wolfee went over to the corner by the pizza place where the bikers hung.

He soon returned, his hands filled with tools. He set about removing the steel plate at the base of the streetlamp.

Inside was a multicolored bird's nest of tightly wound cables, each made up of many smaller wires.

Wolfee looked around almost frantically.

Then he saw what he wanted. He walked over to a park bench which had one plank cracked and loosely screwed into the concrete stanchion. He took hold of it, lifted his foot up against the bench, and tore off about a four foot section of two by four.

He took the board and went back to the streetlamp.

He shoved it behind the tangle of wire at the base of the pole. Then he began to twist. Turn after turn he took up the slack, pulling the guts out of the pole until finally the tearing began. There was crackling and sparks started flying in all directions. More and more of them spraying all around Wolfee like a giant dud Roman candle on the Fourth of July. Then, as the shower of sparks let up, there was a white cloud of smoke that came billowing out of the pole until Wolfee was lost in it.

That's when it happened.

The light flickered. Once, twice, and then, *poof*—the light went out.

And then, a moment after, another light about fifty feet or so down the path flickered, and it too went out. Then the next in line. And the next.

Freddy D, as well as the other inhabitants of the park,

started to make noise and cheer as the chain reaction plunged half the low income housing project into darkness.

They had taken back the night.

The cloud of smoke began to disperse like the aftermath on a battlefield.

At the center of it all stood Wolfee, his hands still gripping the piece of wood. His hair seemed to be standing on end. Smoke was coming from his clothes. He looked over at his main man Freddy D and gave him a big smile—before he fell like a stiff, flat on his face.

~~~

Chapter 2

The handsome gifts that fate and nature lend us
Most often are the very ones that end us.

—*Chaucer*

The story got better each time Spokes told it. It was bound to be a classic in the annals of the neighborhood folklore: *The Night Wolfee Blacked Out the Projects*. Spokes had a way of adding stuff each time he told it. What started out as a three minute story was enhanced—there was now a ten minute version. He was real funny when he told stories. He had a flare for it.

What made him so good at telling stories was the way he could do voices. He was real good at doing voices.

He had Wolfee down to a *T*, that intimidating raspy near-whisper. The words ran at you from the side of his mouth; he ended every phrase, whatever he was saying, leaning in your face, like he was waiting for an answer.

Wolfee didn't mind being mimicked—the most sincere form of flattery and all that... He even liked the story, especially the part about how he tore the board from the bench with his bare hands and how he kept ripping out the wires even after the

15

sparks started flying. Wolfee liked anything that helped to spread his reputation as a tough guy.

Had he heard the long version, he wouldn't't've liked it at all, especially the part of where Spokes told how Rosey called him out: "'Someone fucks with my man Freddy D, they fuck with me. You mess wit da Wolfee, you messin' wit one bad motherfucker.' ...*Pow!* 'You got a problem, Wolfee?' '...No, Rosey, no problem.... What's that, Rosey? You want me to hold him up while you hit him again. Nooo problem.'"

It was amazing to hear Spokes imitate Wolfee and Rosey, both. He'd switch from one to the other like a born schizo. Only he had to be careful—Wolfee didn't like being laughed at. Spokes made sure to change the story a little if he was around.

Once, Spokes was telling it and out of nowhere Wolfee was there.

Wolfee interjected running commentary and in the process, became an unwitting straight man.

"They're going to give me the electric chair one of these days anyway. This was just practice," Wolfee boasted, his short sleeve shirt rolled up high to show off his tattoo—a wolf howling at the moon, the name *Wolfee* inscribed beneath.

Spokes rolled up his sleeves, flexed his small biceps and with the same raspy hyper inflection he added, "I got so many fried brain cells. What's a few more?"

It was hard to tell who did a better Wolfee—Wolfee or Spokes?

Early evening was as light as day but with a full moon sitting pretty and white in a jaundice sky.

Spokes sat against the fence by the handball courts waiting to play. He was up next. Across the basketball courts, at the other end of the park, he could see the Cadillac pull up to the curb. It was an old one with big fins, black. It was well-known in the neighborhood—that was Joey LaPela's car.

The two Joeys paid regular visits to the park, but still... it always seemed special. They usually didn't stay long. Just long enough to take care of business. For Spokes it was a thrill to see the local *Mafioso*.

Truth be known they were strictly small potatoes—loan-sharking, extortion. They were newcomers to the rackets. Associates, not *made* guys. Still, in Spokes' eyes the Joeys were the 'real deal'. They held celebrity status. Next to Rosey they were probably the toughest guys in the park.

Nobody was tougher than Rosey. He had the respect of the whole neighborhood. Even the Joeys wouldn't want to go up against Rosey.

And that was fast becoming their biggest problem—some things you end up learning the hard way.

Spokes watched as Bonj, Joey Bonjonela, got out of the car first and stood there for a minute before LaPela got out. That was the way it was done. Bonj was the bodyguard. A brick shithouse with a Buster Brown haircut. It looked silly, but

17

probably no one ever mentioned that to Bonj. It was common knowledge that Bonj carried a gun with him at all times. LaPela was said to be the nephew of one of the bosses of one of the five families.

Spokes got on his bike and rode toward that side of the park. He wasn't planning on riding right up to LaPela or anything dumb like that. He was just going to head toward the park house... to get a closer look. See what was happening.

Then something wild happened—Bonj waved him over.

Spokes looked around. There was no one else he could have been motioning to, only him.

What could Bonj want with him? He had no idea. *Imagine having Bonj and LaPela as friends.* Spokes' standing in the community would go up instantly if it was thought that he was up-tight with the two Joeys. Nobody would mess with him then.

Despite all that, Spokes maintained his own tough, don't-give-a-fuck attitude. He rode his bike up to Bonj real fast. Then at the last minute he hit the brakes hard and spun out, barely missing him.

Bonj didn't flinch.

"Yeah, what do you want?"

Bonj didn't answer, LaPela did. He had a porkpie hat pushed forward on his forehead; his longish hair, tucked behind his ears, gathered on his collar in back. He was wearing one of those sport shirts with an alligator on it. The likeness was uncanny.

"Spokes, Joey and I want to hear you tell the story about what happened the other night... between Rosey and that guy..."

Bonj filled in the blank, "...Freddy D."

Willy had never spoken to LaPela before. He was surprised and flattered that LaPela even knew his name.

"Would you do that for us...?" LaPela wasn't really asking. He had to know that Spokes would be only too glad to tell him the story. He was being polite. He seemed like a real nice guy.

Spokes launched into his Rosey impersonation...

LaPela listened with growing astonishment. His face cracked a smile.

"Jesus Christ, that sounds just like him...."

Then all of a sudden he got serious; the smile sealed back up. He raised his hand palm-out. Spokes stopped on a dime, mid-sentence.

LaPela asked, "Is that what Rosey said?" He wanted to know, "Is that what Rosey said exactly? that that money wasn't his? that he owed it to other people?"

Spokes' head jiggled.

Bonj mumbled, "That don't mean shit. You can't have one Hebe making his own rules. It don't look right. The rest of the neighborhood ain't dumb. They see what's happening. I'm telling you, you're gonna have to talk to your uncle about that Hebe."

In an aside to Bonj, LaPela talked through his teeth. "Don't tell me what I have to do. You're the one's chickenshit. Maybe I oughta get 'that Hebe' to take over your job. It would seem that he's better at it than you are."

When he turned back toward Willy, the smile was back. "Go on, Kid, do some more..."

Spokes had to think a minute to find his place; he went on with the story.

LaPela laughed in all the right places. "...See how the kid does that twitchy thing with his eyebrows and spits between his teeth... and every other sentence he ends with 'You understand?' ...Sounds just like him. Close your eyes," he told Bonj, "it's just like Rosey was right here in front of us."

"Yeah, it's remarkable." Bonj was making an effort to sound like he gave a fuck. It wasn't working.

"Don't mind Bonjonela, Kid. He don't have no appreciation for the arts... and what's more, he don't have no sense a' humor."

Bonj said something to LaPela in Italian. LaPela said something back. Spokes didn't understand a word.

"You're part Italian, Kid, aren't you?" LaPela didn't wait for Spokes to answer, "On your mother's side?"

Spokes nodded keenly.

"Yeah, that's what I thought. Listen, do yourself a favor, stay clear of *stronzo* like Freddy D... and Wolfee. You know? *Stronzo...?* It means *piece of shit...* Like them two guys... *stronzo*. Don't waste your time with them. They're stupid. Now if you'll excuse us, Spokes, Bonj and I got things to discuss."

Willy wasn't finished telling the story, but then again... it seemed he was. He bumped his bike up the curb, through the hole in the fence, and onto the softball field. He did a wheelie across the yard. He thought the two Joeys must be watching how cool he was. But he didn't want to turn around to check. That wouldn't be cool.

When he got to the handball courts he did turn back—in time to see the taillights on the Caddy's big fins as it squeezed down the narrow street, away from the park.

Spokes could forget about handball. It had gotten too dark. So he rode around in the outfield for a while, doing some fancy flatland freestylin'.

And as the night took hold, it was fast approaching the peak hours for the predominant recreational activity at the park— getting high. At the start of every evening the park would get busy. But then, once everyone had scored, the park was no longer the place to be. It grew depressing. So the thing to do was to stop at the park, score some shit, shoot the bull for an hour or so, and then take off. Maybe come back later when it was real late, like three in the morning; bullshit some more, end up at the Utica Diner. Guys who just stayed in the park all night long— they were losers with no place else to go, too stoned to go anywhere anyway. They'd fall out on a park bench. Wasted.

It was after ten when Spokes rode by Freddy D and Wolfee sitting on a park bench. They were laughing and sharing a quart bottle of malt liquor—*gangster brew* as they liked to call it. There they were, bent over, plotting their revenge on Rosey. Somehow, in their inebriated state, they had actually concocted an ingenious scheme. It was nuts, of course; juvenile, and probably impossible to pull off... but, in its own peculiar way, it really was kind of clever. And what's more, it was funny.

"Hey, Dudes, what you doing?" Spokes asked, slowing to a stop in front of them.

"Come 'ere, Shithead, we wanna ask you a favor," Freddy D said. His face looked lopsided from where Rosey had tagged him.

Spokes leaned over closer, to hear what Freddy had to say.

"Gotya, you little—" Freddy faked a sudden lunge, stopped short, loudly slapping his foot down on the ground.

Spokes reacted, trying to push-off, backup, and peddle away. He got tangled and went down.

Freddy and Wolfee laughed like jackals.

"You fucks!" It was a hard fall and tears were starting to well up in his eyes. He got up quickly and rode away, back to the handball courts.

He was sitting there feeling bad when he saw Freddy D and Wolfee coming toward him. They were still both able to walk, but then it was still early. Wolfee was shouldering his ghetto blaster and the two of them were still laughing like they were demented. Spokes got on his bike.

"Hey, Spokes, my man, don't go nowhere. Freddy and me, we're sorry we laughed at you before. Ain't we, Freddy? No, really! We came over to say we're sorry. We want to make it up to you."

Freddy had a bottle of gangster brew in his hand. He wiped the mouthpiece on his shirt sleeve and held it out to Spokes. "C'mon, Spokes, I didn't fuckin' mean for you to get hurt. You're my friend."

Spokes was skeptical, poised to ride.

"C'mon, Spokes, be a fuckin' man. Drink with us."

Spokes never drank gangster brew before, but he wasn't

going to tell these guys that. He took a long pull.

"You got a cigarette?"

"For my man, Spokes. Here, take a few for later." Wolfee took a handful of cigarettes out of his pack and put them in Spokes' shirt pocket. "What are you doing tonight, Bro? You want to go drinking with me and *D*-man?" Wolfee lit up a joint, took a hit, and passed it to Spokes—not to Freddy—but to Spokes. Freddy didn't say anything; he grinned and patted Spokes on the back.

This was turning out to be a night of firsts. He took a long hit on the fat '*J*,' making a lot of noise, like you're supposed to, like the broken air hose at the gas station where he filled his bike tires. "Good weed," he spoke from the top of his throat, holding his breath, holding down the smoke. It burned and he coughed.

"Here you go, take a drink, you'll be alright."

This was pretty cool, hanging out with Freddy D and Wolfee. He was like one of the boys.

"So, what do you say? We're going over to the liquor store to get another bottle. You coming?"

"Fuck yeah, he's comin'," Freddy D insisted. He had his hand on the handlebars and was pulling at the bike before Spokes could agree. And the three of them were off on the well-traveled path from the park to the liquor store.

The other stores on the block were all closed up tight with double security gates across the front. The liquor store was the one oasis of activity on a sidewalk going nowhere. The three homeboys sat outside passing a bottle of gangster brew and a joint.

Spokes was awful high by now. And Wolfee started to explain the plan...

Meanwhile, Freddy had walked over to the payphone alongside the building. He was dialing for a while, obviously not getting through, but then he would just hang up and dial again.

"Spokes, my man, I want you to listen to someone..." Wolfee changed the station on the radio and Spokes found himself listening to the voice of a pleasant-enough sounding woman. "Spokes, my man, we are listening to my psych-ologist. You know that I am certifiably criminally insane?" He looked at Spokes, waiting for an answer.

"Sure, Wolfee, everybody knows that."

Wolfee smiled broadly.

"This here lady psych-ologist is out-a'-sight. This is Dr. Leslie Gift, my radio shrink. You ever listen to Dr. Gift?"

"No, I never—"

"Well, you ought to. She's a smart lady. And besides, she's got a sexy fuckin' voice. Listen to that voice."

Wolfee moved the radio closer to Spokes and turned the volume up a little. He cocked his head to the side and looked right at Spokes, waiting for his response.

"Yeah, she's got a real nice voice.... I bet she's real pretty."

Dr. Gift's soothing voice had a lulling effect on Spokes' by-now-easily-malleable consciousness. He was not aware of it, but his body registered a certain kinship with the voice. It was a controlled voice, a highly skilled voice, especially when

24

juxtaposed with Wolfee's rapid-fire delivery leaning in his face, outlining that "little favor" that he and Freddy needed to ask of their "good buddy" Spokes....

From out of the box, Dr. Gift was speaking with a wimpy sounding male caller. The caller was explaining how his marriage was wonderful except that he found himself becoming obsessed with one little thing that his wife did. As he told the story, his voice sounded shaky and scared. His wife, he said, yelled at him every time he used the dish towel in the kitchen to wipe his hands. It really got to him. He was a jumpy nervous wreck every time he walked into his own kitchen. If he was anywhere near the dish towel, his whole body would go tense. It was having a negative effect on his marriage. He was going to have to leave her. He didn't know what else to do.

"Now let me understand this." Her voice was businesslike, but with a caring tone reaching out to understand. "How big a woman is your wife? I guess what I'm trying to find out here is, Why are you so afraid of her yelling at you? Are you afraid of her physically harming you? Is that it?"

"Oh, no," the caller stammered, "she's a tiny thing, ninety-five pounds soaking wet."

"Well, then aren't you pathetic!" Dr. Gift's tone of voice and the fact that she had phrased her statement as a question made what she said sound almost inoffensive. She remained even and sweet as she told the caller "You're just looking for something to make your life—and what's worse, her life—miserable. If you're going to leave her, then just do it and stop driving her crazy in the process. But you're not going to do that either. You know why?—because you're not a man. Does a man act like this? Well... tell me, Does he?"

"No, I guess not." The caller seemed to want to agree with her.

"You guess not! Just listen to yourself. You don't sound at all angered that I just said you're not a man. You have a more serious problem than that dish towel. You're the problem. You're the dish towel. And you like being one. I suggest you get into some therapy. In the meanwhile, keep two separate dish towels in the kitchen or switch to paper towels. Good luck and thanks for calling.

"It's time again for me to remind out listeners that you are listening to the Mutual Broadcasting System. Our show is heard live, weeknights from eleven to one, and for those of you who can't stay up late, or if you've missed any part of tonight's show, be sure to tune in tomorrow—on Saturday and Sunday afternoons KCBS features 'The Best of Dr. Leslie Gift' from four to six; we'll be rebroadcasting the highlights of the weeks programs. I hope you'll be listening. And right now, if any of our listeners out there want to call in, the number is 1-800-395-7755. It's a toll free call. You will speak first with Jerry, our show's producer. When you speak to Jerry, please give him only your first name and your age—we think it's important that we place you in the proper life passage. Be as brief as possible and try to present your problem in the form of a question. Please remember, we are only a radio show. We cannot realistically deal with major life problems. However, within the limited time and format, we hope to inform and entertain, and, as I like to say, we try, in some small way, to make your already good life a little better. Please turn down your radio when you get on the air. And now, to our next caller. Hello, you are on the air.... Rose, are you there?"

Wolfee had explained the plan to Spokes. And the way he explained it, it was a joke, just a crazy practical joke.

In the interim Freddy had gotten through on the phone; he was obviously talking to someone. All of a sudden, Freddy covered the receiver with one hand and began waving frantically with the other.

Wolfee had Spokes by the arm, up and over to the phone.

Again, Dr. Gift said, "Rose, hello, are you there?"

"Quick." Freddy pushed the phone toward Spokes. "Okay, do it. Make like you're Rosey."

Spokes just stood there holding his hand over the mouthpiece while his eyes tried to focus. He was suddenly aware of how unsteady he was on his feet.

"Hurry, she's waiting. Tell her your name is Rosey and you're 26 years old."

Spokes slowly moved his hand off the phone and, speaking through a tightly clenched jaw, said, "The name's Rosey, not Rose." He raised his eyebrows and spit between his teeth, then quickly covered up the phone and looked for approval at Freddy and Wolfee.

They loved it. They patted Spokes on the back. Their smiles

were illuminated in the unsavory light that strayed from the liquor store. Everything was growing a little fuzzy at the edges. Spokes looked over at Wolfee and began laughing uncontrollably. This was so preposterous.

"It's just a joke, a practical joke," Wolfee told him. "C'mon, tell her what I said."

At the other end of the line, they could hear Dr. Gift saying, "Oh my, I am sorry. It does happen on occasion that when Jerry hands me the note with the name of our next caller, sometimes, if it's an unusual name, I mispronounce it or, as in this case, get it totally wrong. Do forgive me. Now, Rosey, you are still with me?"

Spokes still had the receiver to his ear and his hand over the mouthpiece. Freddy's lopsided face grinned at him sideways as he slowly lifted his hand off.

"Like I said, the name is Rosey, and I'm 26 years old. Rosey's not my real name, just a nickname. It has nothing to do with anything, you understand?"

"Alright, Rosey, and how can I help you tonight?"

~~~

Chapter 3

It takes your enemy and your friend, working together, to hurt you to the heart; the one to slander you and the other to get the news to you.

—*Mark Twain*

Spokes glided up to the window counter of the pizza parlor across from the park. It was almost four o'clock on a muggy overcast day after... It was almost time for the rebroadcast of "The Dr. Leslie Gift Show." Wolfee had been telling everyone to listen in to KCBS Talk Radio, 74.9 AM, starting at 3 p.m.—that there was going to be something special that they wouldn't want to miss. Wolfee made Spokes promise not to tell anyone about it. Said he wanted it should be a surprise. ...For the next several minutes at least, it was a secret. A terrible secret.

"Hey, George, gimme a slice of Sicilian." He slapped five quarters down on the counter. "The corner piece."

"Anything on a-top? Sausage?"

"Nope."

George slid the pizza cutter between the slices and then pulled off the corner square. It was a generous portion. He flipped open the oven and tossed it in. Then he turned and

29

looked at Spokes. It was hot behind those ovens. There were beads of sweat standing out on his face; the front of his apron was caked with flour and stained with tomato sauce. He had to weigh better than two hundred pounds and he wasn't much taller than Spokes.

Spokes looked at the clock on the Budweiser sign, then back at the fat pizza man. "Hey, George, how come you changed your radio station? You never listen to talk radio."

"Wolfee make-a me listen to his a-radio—how you say?—psych-ologist? He tell-a me that there's a-gonna be something I should a-hear. You know what's this something?"

"Beats me." Spokes picked at a patch of gum stuck to his front tire. Then, changing the subject, "George, you married?"

"Gonna be a-ten years this September."

"No shit! You got any kids?"

"I got two girls."

Spokes shook his head in disbelief. "That's amazing, a fat guy like you."

"What's a-matter you? You crazy kid. Here, take-a you pizza and go bother somebody else.... It's a-hot, so be careful you don't burn-a you fool mouth."

A line of motorcycles stretched across the curb in front of the park. Spokes bumped onto the sidewalk and came to a stop in front of Wolfee and Freddy D.

"Hey, you little fuckface, give me a bite." Freddy mumbled like he had marbles in his mouth. His face was still swollen and discolored on the side. It wasn't only black and blue; it was turning an ugly greenish brown.

"Ask nice and I might just give you some."

Freddy rolled his eyes like he was asking heaven for patience and he said, "Pleeeese."

"Okay, but just one bite."

"I promise, just one bite."

Spokes held out the slice. Before he could pull it back, Freddy opened his mouth as wide as he could and tore off almost the entire slice in one bite. Chewing and laughing, pizza was falling out of his face. Spokes was left holding crust.

"You son-of-a-bitch! You're gonna buy me another slice." He threw the crust at Freddy who was busy stiffing his mouth. "I hope you choke on it, you fuck."

Suddenly, some kind of commotion broke out behind them, in the street. All heads turned.

Animal, a neighborhood biker, was yelling at some old guy.

What had happened was this: Animal had been cruising on his trike, the old guy and his wife were driving in their blue Buick behind him—Animal said they were tailgating. More than likely Animal was going too slow or maybe the old guy wanted to get a closer look at the weirdo on the strange machine. Animal was by far the scariest looking guy around. Covered with tattoos, wearing a dungaree jacket with the sleeves cut off, a skull on the back—he had a cowbell earring dangling from his left ear. But he wasn't nearly as tough as he looked. That would have been impossible. Truth was, Animal was a scaredy-cat when it came to picking on anyone his own size. But since there weren't many his size, he found plenty of opportunity to push his weight around. But he waited till he was in front of the park to get brave with an old man in a blue Buick. He stopped his trike, jumped off and started yelling, "You been on my ass for the past mile. What's your fucking problem. You one of these motherfuckers likes to run bikers off the road?"

The poor old guy was turning white as a sheet. Animal wasn't the only one yelling at him; his wife was panicked. "Roll up the window, Herbert, quickly," she shrieked.

Animal kept hollering, "You picked the wrong guy to fuck with." He could smell the fear. He was used to the smell, only this time it wasn't coming off his own fat ass. He made a grab as though he was going to reach into the window, but it closed too soon. It was a slow move, even for Animal. He wasn't so intent at getting at the old man as he was at making a lot of noise and getting the attention of his cronies in the park. And he was succeeding.

Someone yelled, "Hey, Animal's in trouble. Let's go!" Someone else yelled, "That tailgating motherfucker! Break his fucking head, Animal."

This was just what the afternoon needed, a little excitement. The park emptied in under a minute, forming a half-crazy mob around the blue Buick. They started rocking the car from side to side, harder and harder, until the wheels were tipping off the ground. A few of the boys went to their cars to get tire irons and chains. Next thing you know, Animal jumps onto the hood, yelling and cursing and doing a little dance to keep his balance as the car's being bounced around. He raised up his foot and for a moment it looked like he was going to smash his steel-toed boot into the windshield when someone grabbed hold of his other leg and yanked him down.

It was Wolfee.

Now it was Animal's turn to exude the stink of fear. Wolfee had him pinned flat against the ground, Animal's eyes searching madly for a way out.

"Wolfee, what's wrong? Come on. Let go." Animal would never intentionally fuck with Wolfee. Not many would. He was bad news.

"That's my aunt in that car."

"Wolfee, I didn't know. How was I to know?"

Animal started to cringe, anticipating a powerful punch in the face. He'd open his eyes, see Wolfee raise up his fist, close his eyes, then open them again and see the fist waving inches from his face, then close them again. This went on for a while until Wolfee finally let go the collar of Animal's jacket and got up off of him.

Wolfee went over to the trike, put it in neutral, and pushed it to the side of the road.

"Go ahead. Get outta here." He waved the car through; the crowd moved aside.

"Hey, that wasn't your aunt...?" Freddy D wanted to know.

Now that Animal was on his feet and no longer had Wolfee's hand at his throat, he didn't quite believe that bit about "the aunt" either. But he wasn't going to say anything. Freddy D, on the other hand, was Wolfee's main man. Besides, he was tough. Maybe even tougher than Wolfee.

"This is a place of business. You act like a bunch of kids, you're going to bring the heat... over something stupid like this." Wolfee was speaking real loud so everyone could hear. So they would know his reason for stopping their fun.

And he was right. If they'd have busted up that old couple and their car, the cops would've busted up the park. There would be no more hang out for awhile. Suddenly it made sense to everyone.

Except Freddy D, who still wanted to know, "But that wasn't really your aunt, was it?"

Wolfee looked embarrassed by his friend. Under his breath he answered him, "No, that wasn't my fucking aunt."

Freddy laughed and sounded pleased with himself: "I knew that wasn't your aunt."

Meanwhile, though the ruckus was over, the crowd wasn't disbursing. It felt good to form a mob—strong and protected. They weren't ready to disband. Everyone mulled around, caught up in the illusion that something was happening. All the various factions—older guys, younger guys, bikers, broads, dopers, gamblers—just standing around in the street.

That's when Wolfee yelled, "Hey, everybody, listen up! Ain't that Rosey on the radio?"

"Hey, turn it up," someone shouted as they began to crowd around Wolfee's ghetto blaster.

The stereo speakers in Mustang Sally's souped-up '67

fastback—white with blue racing stripes down the middle—were tuned in.

And when Sal turned up the volume, the whole park got to hear the voice of Rosey confessing his deepest, darkest secret to Dr. Leslie Gift, radio psychologist:

Rosey: I got a problem, Dr. Gift. You see, I just found out... I'm a queer. I'm afraid everyone else is going to find out.

Dr. Gift: Now let me understand this. You say you're 26 years old, and you're just now realizing—for the first time—that you are a homosexual.

Rosey: Yeah, that's right. I'm a homo.

Dr. Gift: Rosey, I want you to know that it is not unusual for someone your age to discover his homosexuality. There is some debate among health care professionals whether this condition is a result of upbringing or if some people are born different. Let's put that aside for the time being. Tell me more about why *you* think you're gay. What made *you* suddenly decided that you're gay? Have you had girlfriends in the past? Did you ever date women?

Rosey: Oh sure, I used to go out with a lot of women.

Dr. Gift: And were you at all attracted by them?

Rosey: You want to know if I got hard with women?

Dr. Gift: Well, it's not that simple, Rosey. You see, all of us have some aspects of the opposite sex within us. There are gay men who are husbands and even fathers. In that respect, sexual orientation is a matter of—

Rosey: I was impotent with women.

Dr. Gift: Oh... I see. You've *never* been able to get an erection with a woman.

Rosey: Never. Only when I'm around guys.

Dr. Gift: Oh... I see. So now you have a lover and you're worried that people might find out, is that it?

Rosey: That's part of it. The man I love, he doesn't even know how I feel. And I'm afraid to let him know because I don't want to be found out, you understand? I got a reputation in my neighborhood, and if people found out, well...

Dr. Gift: Now wait a minute. Let me get this straight—no pun intended. You haven't even discussed this with this man whom you *supposedly* love. Do you even know if *he* is homosexual?

Rosey: Well... no, I'm not sure... but I think he—

Dr. Gift: Stop right there! Before you go on and say anything else, I think the first thing you have to do is talk to this man. Let him know how you feel. However—and I cannot stress this enough—you must be very careful how you approach this other man on this subject. If he's not receptive, you must let it go. You don't know for sure that he's gay. If he is, then I wish you good luck. Be discreet and if people find out—well that's just something you're going to have to deal with when and if it happens. You're calling from a big city. I think you'll find that people are more tolerant than you think.

Rosey: But there's something else I didn't tell you.... The man I love, his name is George, he's a pizza man, and he's fat—I seem to be attracted to fat men. Not only am I ashamed that I'm queer, but I'm embarrassed by how fat George is, you understand?

Dr. Gift: I understand that you have a lot of growing up to do. For a 26 year old, you have an extremely immature concept of love. Instead of worrying about how fat George is, you're going to have to learn to accept yourself. I suspect you're going to need some kind of therapy to do that. Now if you want to stay on the line, Jerry will have some referrals for you in your area. We're going to go to a break now. This is the Mutual Broadcasting System.

~~~

Chapter 4

...to be angry with the right person to the right extent and at the right time and with the right object and in the right way—that is not easy...

—*Aristotle*

Rosey was a street fightin' hero to the neighborhood. Not only to Spokes. Stories of his fights were told and retold. So it was completely understandable that there should be a wounded hush over the crowd at the park that day. How could this be the same Rosey who, when he was only fifteen, got into a fight with three sailors at the same time?—and won. The same Rosey who, at age seventeen, fought in the Golden Gloves?—and now he's supposed to be a *fairy*. It did not go down well. People don't like it when you destroy their heroes. Uneasy laughter spread like a fart in an elevator on a long ride down.

For a minute there even Spokes felt somehow betrayed by the news....

But that didn't make any sense. After all, he knew it wasn't Rosey. Damned if he didn't respect Rosey more than just about anyone. He couldn't stand by and let this happen.

Spokes got up on the hood of a parked car. "Yeah, that's

right." He raised his eyebrows and he spit between his teeth. "I'm a homo. You understand? What of it? You gonna make something of it?"

And suddenly—like the news delivery truck tossing a bundle of papers onto the sidewalk with a thud—it dawned on everyone. That was the voice on the radio, that was the Rosey they'd been listening to. They'd been had. How foolish they all felt! How relieved! The nervous snickers relaxed, a gale of laughter burst forth. They laughed at the prank and at themselves and at young Willy Freeman doing his shtick like a pint-sized James Cagney.

"You got a problem wit dat?" He spoke through a tightly clenched jaw. He clenched his fists and lowered his head. "Yeah... you. What'd you say?" He held out his hand hip-high palm down and snapped his fingers, pointing at his audience. "I'm talking to you. You got a problem wit dat?"

He had them howling.

"Hey, Rosey, how come you like fat boys?" Sally shouted to Spokes, playing along.

"I love fat boys. What's it to you? You got a problem wit dat?"

"No... no problem, Rosey. It's cool." Sal spoke to those around him, "Eddy Rosen can like whatever he wants. Me, I'm going on a diet." He slapped his substantial beer belly and everyone cracked up. Mustang Sally was a funny guy—with his cool-cat goatee and his hot rod Mustang.

Spokes was having such a good time being the center of attention, he almost didn't hear the voice shouting over the crowd: "Hey, you little prick, get down off my car."

It was Campy. Spokes hadn't realize that it was Campy's car he was standing on.

Now Campy, which was short for Campanella, was an easygoing, good-natured sort. Everyone's friend. He wouldn't hurt anyone. But at twenty-six, he had never owned a car before and he had just acquired this jalopy from his brother-in-law. He was pissed.

"Hey, take it easy. I'll get down..." Spokes was through playing the tough guy. He was more sorry than scared. He didn't mean to stand on Campy's car.

He fell hard as Campy pulled him down off the hood. And wound up on the ground, his back scraped against the sidewalk and his head bumped on the metal bumper.

He might have taken even more lumps, but for the brick shithouse who muscled his way between him and Campy.

"That's right. Take it easy." It was Bonj. "Let's nobody get rowdy now."

There'd been so much going on, Spokes hadn't noticed the two Joeys. The Cadillac was parked head-in in the red zone like a law unto itself. From the driver's seat, Joey LaPela watched with apparent interest.

Campy stepped back. He had a very strong sense of self-preservation. He didn't want any part of Bonj.

Spokes put out his hand. Bonj turned away. Apparently he wasn't going to get a hand up.

"So who needs your help anyway?" Spokes stood up and

brushed himself off.

Okay, he thought, *that's enough excitement for one day. If nothing else happens the rest of the month... I've filled my excitement quota.*

But it was a hot afternoon and it wasn't about to cool down. Things were going to get sticky. Rosey was coming down the block.

It got awful quiet as he walked among the gathering by the park entrance.

It was normal for guys to make way for Rosey when he walked past, so maybe he didn't notice anything as a couple guys tripped over their own feet stepping back.

He stopped next to Campy and stood with his back to the chain link fence. Campy was Rosey's friend. Rosey didn't have many friends, not real friends. His eyes darted in their sockets. He took it all in—the row of cars, the line of Harleys, the crowd, LaPela, Bonj, Freddy D, Wolfee.

"So Campy, what do you say? What's going on?" Rosey's chin jerked forward, gesturing at all the people in the street. Then he turned his head to the side and squirted spit between his teeth. He turned back, his eyebrows raised, his stare resting on Campy.

As far back as they went and as good friends as they were, Campy still felt uneasy around Rosey at times. This was one of those times.

"Nothing much, Rosey. Animal and some of his biker buddies got nothing better to do than terrorize some old man. The guy was tailgating his trike. They surrounded his car, shook him up a bit. That's it. Not a whole lot happening... How 'bout

41

with you? Things okay with you?"

"Yeah, fine. Everything's fine."

LaPela was pulling out. Rosey watched the Caddy like he was mad-doggin' it. The car swung around and grumbled away.

"Just wish that guinea bastard would drop dead."

Campanella didn't take offense. He knew none was intended.

"Come on, let's go over to the pizza place. I'll buy you a slice."

"No. Thanks anyway, Rosey, I gotta get going." Campy fidgeted with his keys. "Something I got to do. Besides, I ain't hungry."

"So you'll sit with me while I eat. What have you got to do? You got a hot date or something?"

"No. Got to drive my sister to bingo," he lied. He was not up to hanging out with Rosey tonight. It was just too unnerving. "It's Wednesday night and if she misses her bingo... You know I wouldn't have the car if it wasn't for her. It's almost time, I gotta get going."

"Okay, I'll tell you what—I'll eat later. I'll go with you. We'll drop your sister off, and then head back for some pizza. Or even better, after we drop her off, we get the fuck outta here altogether. We'll take that mean machine of yours into the city, see if we can't—"

"Hey, Rosey, I don't have enough gas—"

"I got money. I'll—"

"—and I'm probably going to have to be around to pick her

42

up after."

"Okay, okay. So we come back here after."

"I don't think that's such a good idea, Rosey. You know Carol. She not exactly a fan of yours. She'd get on my case if you're with me. You know how she is. She got it in her head that you're a bad influence. I just don't want to start. You can understand that, can't you?"

"Yeah, sure. You got wheels and now you don't want to hang out with your old friends anymore." Rosey knew that had nothing to do with it. He also knew that Campy's sister hated his guts. It was no use. Might as well let it go.

Campy didn't say anything for a while. Then he said, "Listen, I gotta go. You wanna lift to the pizza place?"

So the doors of the Campymobile creaked open and they got in. The engine turned over, the exhaust coughed up a puff of fetid black fumes.

It wasn't until the heap was actually rolling away that someone was brave enough to joke, "Rosey's going to go see his sweetheart, fat Georgie."

...Half a block and Rosey hopped out. Campy made a right on the avenue and smudged his way into the sunset.

Sundown was drawing near, the neon pizza sign lit up just as Rosey stepped onto the sidewalk. The door was wedged open. A fan inside strained to push the hot air out, carrying the smell of pizza into the street. No better advertisement than the smell of pizza baking. Rosey hadn't realized how hungry he was. He inhaled and his stomach clamored loudly.

He didn't even eat yet and already he had *agita*.

He was annoyed at Campy. He wouldn't admit it to himself, but he was hurt. And on top of that, he was feeling a little strung out on *smack*. He had a growing *chippy* that not many people knew about. He had growing debts that too many people knew about. And from the vibes he got off the two Joeys, his problems were growing with the *vig*. All in all, he was in a lousy disposition.

And as this one cross customer crossed the doorstep into the pizza parlor on that late afternoon, he was stepping into the annals of local legend. A familiar habitat for the likes of one, Eddy Rosen, alias Rosey. The details of the events which followed are a little sketchy. The place was almost empty except for two *suits* doing up meatball heroes and Budweisers at a back table. No waiter, it was a small place. Most of the sales took place at the window counter. If you were there for a sit-down meal, George would bring your order to your table. According to the popular version of the story, Rosey asked fat George for an order of lasagna with his sweet Italian sausage on the side. That's how it appeared on the menu—sweet Italian sausage. Next thing you know, fat George is telling Rosey what he thinks of *son-of-a-bitch pervert faggots like a-him.*

There's a breed of predator which gives little or no warning before it strikes. The pit bull is like that, none of its ferociousness dissipated in the bark or the growl. Eddy Rosen was like that. The poor pizza man didn't know what hit him. Pulling his fist up from his hip like a gunfighter on a quick draw, Rosey laid into that oversized gut with an upper cut he aimed at George's backbone. It made a thud like a fastball in a catcher's mitt.

The two men at the back table looked up from their meatball sandwiches.

Before the pizza man could recover, Rosey was all over him. Three or four quick punches in the face pushed him back against the pizza ovens. Then he reached up and grabbed George by the hair and started to slam his head against the oven door.

It would have been all over for fat George if it hadn't been for the two guys in the back. It turned out that they were plainclothes cops. It all happened so fast. The cops were on their feet in a matter of seconds. Lucky for George.

What exactly happened next was to become a point of contention in the legal proceedings which were to arise from the conduct of the arresting officers. It seems that initially the officers failed to identify themselves as police. Maybe they were doing some undercover work and they thought they'd be able to break it up without having to blow their cover to the whole neighborhood. Two of them, one of him—break up the fight, rough him up a little, send him on his way. Should've been simple enough. They'd sort it out later. The more urgent matter at hand was to save the pizza man before his head was pounded as flat as his pizza dough.

Officers LeDoux and Moody were only recently partnered. Moody was the veteran detective—older, more sure of himself. LeDoux was only out of uniform a short time. He was assigned to LeDoux so he could pick up a few pointers from the "old pro." Not that Moody was old. He was the kind of guy who it's hard to guess his age. He could have been 35 or he could have been 45. He was clean shaven, neat, and trim. He could pass for an executive who stayed in shape playing tennis at the country club. At first glance, you'd say he was a polite, gentle man. Nothing could have been further from the truth. John Moody was a fowl-mouth, ill-tempered misanthrope. And LeDoux was finding it hard to take. But when the situation arose calling for a coordinated effort, any tension between the two men ceased to exist.

"That's enough. Let him go." Moody spoke with such authority that when the assailant didn't so much as bat an eye, it should have registered that something wasn't right.

LeDoux took Moody's lead and using his decidedly intimidating size, he came forward. "He said, 'That's enough.' Now let him go."

Still, it had no impact on Rosey who took only a brief break to shoot a contemptuous look at the pair—"Stay out of it"— before he went back to the business of banging George's head.

LeDoux moved in with his arms outstretched ready to grab hold. But before his arms could encircle him, Rosey's fists were making bone-cracking contact with his ribs. He must have taken seven or eight punches all in the same exact spot before he finally took a step back. His ruddy complexion went bloodless as he collapsed to his knees gasping for air.

Rosey started to smile. A good brawl was just what he needed. He was in his element now. All his worldly problems were left behind.

Detective Moody took it all in—the smile, the stance, the arms waving like two jackhammers. It was becoming increasingly clear—he had misread the situation.

His hand was reaching into his jacket for his gun and his mouth was opening to say *POLICE OFFICER*. The words never got out, just a garbled mouthful of syllables stifled by a knuckle sandwich. There was no pain, not yet. That would come later. But Moody wasn't thinking about later. He had to deflect the next blow. At eye level, the fist waved ever so slightly, measuring him for a big right hand. His brain frantically telegraphed messages to his arms, but they weren't getting through. He couldn't move. The fist crashed into his open jaw, knocking the mandible off its condyles. Some teeth came loose in his mouth and blood splattered across his face. Somehow, he was still on his feet. Rosey steadied him with one hand and lined him up with the other. He pulled his fist back, but before it could fly, fat George dropped him with a rolling pin.

Which was just as well, because LeDoux had managed to unholster his gun.

Fat George may have saved Rosey's life.

He definitely saved Detective Moody's face. But only a little. He'd already lost face. How could he let one guy do this!

They dragged Rosey out and into an unmarked car in the alley behind the stores. In minutes two squad cars and an ambulance had arrived. A crowd was gathering outside the pizza place.

As Spokes rode up to the cluster of flashing lights, the car carrying Rosey was pulling out of the driveway. He had come to and was sitting in the back with his hands cuffed behind him. He stared out the window and though his eyes were looking straight at Spokes, he didn't seem to be seeing him. All the same, it scared Spokes half to death.

~~~

Chapter 5

Nobody loves creditors and dead men.

—Ugo Betti

North of the projects on Ralph Avenue, trains with a hundred cars attached rolled into the Brooklyn Terminal Market. Under the El, on the street behind the poultry market where the smell makes people walk fast, Wolfee loitered in the shadows. After dark this stretch of avenue was deserted. The city hadn't bothered to replace the old-fashioned streetlamps; they brushed eerie yellow varnish over everything. The street was full of potholes and the big-finned Caddy did a slow rock and roll.

Bonj had come alone.

"*Pee-yew,* it stinks," he said. "Get in…. So what's this about us having something to talk about?"

Bonj didn't like Wolfee and the feeling was mutual. But lately they had something in common—someone they both didn't like.

"Bonj, you know who I just saw?—Rosey. He's outta jail."

"Yeah, I know…. You didn't get me out here to tell me that. Whadaya want?"

At the root of the animosity between Wolfee and Bonj—two classic ingredients: fear and jealousy.

Wolfee had a sneaking suspicion that he could take Bonj, that Bonj wasn't all he was cracked up to be. That was just how he felt. And when Wolfee felt something, he was transparent. Bonj could see that Wolfee wasn't intimidated by him, and that made him uncomfortable. And when Bonj was uncomfortable, he puffed himself up like a thorny blowfish.

Wolfee shifted in his seat, like he was trying it on for size. Black leather interior—nice. There was a rumor that the doors and windows were bulletproof. It supposedly used to belong to LaPela's uncle, Don Tjipani. Wolfee could see himself now—Mafia enforcer. Some men dream of giving orders—top dog, Mr. Big; that never entered Wolfee's head. When he let himself visualize—the way Dr. Gift says—his perfect place in life, it was always as number 2 man, the stalwart soldier.

Patience wasn't one of Bonj's strong qualities: "So...? What's up? I ain't got all night."

"I want a loan."

"Really? ...And what kinda money we talkin' about?"

Wolfee told him what he had in mind; Bonj looked at him cockeyed. "Whadaya want wit dat kinda money?"

"Is that a condition for my getting the loan? I gotta tell you what I want it for?"

"Nah. Banks ask question. All I gotta know is, When do you need it and for how long?"

...So it was arranged.

And Wolfee was into the Joeys deep over his head.

"One other thing..." Bonj added before he drove off and left Wolfee on the street that smelled of plucked chickens, "Why meet here? What's wrong wit the park, like a normal human being?"

That reminded Wolfee, it was very important that he be clear on this next point: "I don't want anybody to know about this."

Bonj gave him his bored-and-disgusted look, which was only slightly different from his regular all-the-time look. "Just make your payments or else that'll be the least of your worries."

"Hey, I'm serious about this. I got my reasons." Wolfee was leaning into the open window, his index finger waving in front of Bonj's nose. "Anybody finds out... and it's off."

"Hey, nobody'll find out... unless you tell 'em. Privileged communication—just like a priest or a lawyer... or, in your case, a psychiatrist. Now get your finger outta my face before I break it."

He hung a U-turn.

Wolfee was again alone behind the poultry slaughterhouse. You can get used to a bad smell, like when your eyes adjust to the dark. When he first got there he had to take shallow breaths to keep from gagging. Now he hardly noticed it. And his mind was elsewhere. There were no thoughts of Bonj, or of the money to be paid back. There was only the look he was going to see on Freddy D's face when he handed him the money. He'd be sure not to make a big deal out of it. No big deal. He would simply explain how he had had a talk with Rosey, after which Rosey decided to return Freddy's money. *Nothing to it. ...And oh, by the way, Freddy, if you should see Rosey, best not to mention it. No need to rub it in. Rosey has enough problems these days.* Chances are Freddy D wouldn't go near Rosey anyway. Not after what Rosey did to him. But everything was going to be alright now. Wolfee was going to make sure of it. They'd score big and Wolfee would use his share to pay back Bonj. ...Or maybe he wouldn't even pay Bonj. If Rosey could get away with stiffing the Joeys....

* * * *

A day later, the body of Freddy D'Vogelieri was carted away off the floor of the IRT. The coroner ruled it an accidental overdose. There was no wallet; it took two days to get a positive ID. Brooklyn Morgue sees a dozen OD's a week. It's morbidly routine, the need for urgency long past.

They didn't know that Wolfee was frantic, looking all over for his main man. ...And his money.

~~~

Chapter 6

Sticks and stones
May break my bones
But words will never
Harm me.

—*Traditional children's rhyme*

Across the street from 1736—the building where Spokes lived—there was a large vacant lot which was simply called *the lots* by everyone in the neighborhood. The lots extended from the junkyards along Flatlands Avenue down to the projects. On the far side, row houses stood under construction. Row upon row of identical multifamily dwellings were behind those. It was inevitable that they should continue their approach, making the lots smaller and smaller until there would be no lots. But in the meantime, the lots was the most communing with nature that a project kid was likely to have.

The entrance to the lots was marked by a huge sickly weeping willow. That old tree had taken more crap than any living thing should have to—pollution in the air and in the soil, the endless noise of the traffic on Ralph Avenue. Its branches

53

were infested with bugs and it made you itchy just to walk under it. The trunk branched off low to the ground. It was so spread out, it had several trunks. Thick roots ran along the ground in all directions, from one trunk to the next. There were two tremendous rocks at its base, like small boulders, each the size of a Volkswagen. There were no other rocks like that anywhere. It was hard to imagine how they got there. Around the rocks was all manner of junk—a rusted out shopping cart, dried out paint cans, a charred mattress, pornographic magazines, and a billion empty beer bottles.

Beyond the ingress, the path wound down past an odd shaped slab of concrete the size of a pickup truck. The rest of the structure was long gone. No one had any idea what it had been. The path continued through tall weeds that would rustle as the rats rushed around. Then it opened onto a clearing. Off to the right, near a lone sycamore, stood a lean-to patched together from sheets of corrugated steel and the wood from orange crates. Inside, on car seats, sat Spokes and Jeffrey Munchik.

Most of the kids that played in the lots were young kids— twelve year olds who would come home at the end of the day covered with dirt and scratches, and airplane glue. Spokes was too old for that stuff.

But some guys don't outgrow a certain phase. They get stuck in it. Jeffrey Munchik was stuck in glue. He was a year older than Spokes and he was still hanging out in the lots. He was really big and he was really dumb. He was king of the glue sniffers.

Besides the fact that Spokes had outgrown all this, it was off limits. From the fifth floor across the street his mom could look out their window and see young boys stumble out of the lots, high from sniffing glue. She had made him promise to stay out of the lots. Good thing they didn't live near the park—that was all the way on the other side of the projects.

But now the park was off limits too. Not because of Mom, because of Rosey. Word was out—he was looking for Spokes.

Fat George wasn't going to press charges. What's more, he backed Rosey, said the cops never identified themselves. He had a business to think of. He didn't want any more trouble. It was all a misunderstanding. *All a-clear up-a now.*

...Except that Spokes was afraid to show his face in the neighborhood anymore.

There was a rumor going around that when Rosey got outta jail, he came straight to the park, got really wasted, and started asking if anybody had seen Spokes.

"Sss... sss... Spokes, what are you g...g...going to do? You ca... ca... can't hide from Rosey forever." Munchik had a speech impediment. Given the gems inclined to roll off his tongue, it was a step in the right direction.

"Munch, I wish I knew."

"If this Rosey guy really is a fag like you said... maybe, if you slap him hard, he'll cry like a girl. That's what happens if you slap a fag. He'll cry just like a girl." Munchik stuttered through his *slap-a-fag* scenario while stirring a fresh quart of Weldwood Contact Cement.

Munchik didn't live in the projects. He never hung out at the park. And he didn't know Rosey. He didn't know *shit*.

"Munch, I told you, Rosey's no fag. I just *said* he was a fag. It was a joke.... Oh, what's the use! Never mind."

Telling Munch to never mind was like telling an ostrich to never fly. Not much need for concern there.

Munch was busy pouring the yellow *goo* into two number 9 brown paper bags in the exact same way he had done a hundred times before. The bags were doubled. He was careful not to get any on the sides. He rolled the top of one bag into a cuff and fitted it to his face. He made sure it covered his mouth and nose and no air could get in. He breathed a few times and the bag crinkled closed and puffed back out. He passed the bag to Spokes, then poured more glue into the other bag for himself.

What the heck! Spokes leaned forward and settled in for an afternoon in dreamland.

It had been a while. And with glue... it's something else altogether. Even if you do it all the time, you're never ready for it. Those who know will tell you: acid aside, there's nothing else that puts you out there like glue. No smoke. Not junk. Nothing. A dollar thirty-nine and you got the keys to the cosmos. The combination to unlock the dream cortex.

First you put on a *buzz*. Spokes could hear it. It was like the weeds around them were alive with the sounds of a billion crickets. It grew. Thicker. Louder. Until it was in the air. He could see the sound like the flickering of pulsating dust particles bathed in light. Then he was joined to the oscillating particles all around. It was in him. The buzz. In his body and his head. He could feel himself slipping into a dream.

Across the avenue, the curtains on the fifth story window moved aside as Helene Freeman looked out at the lots. She had seen him go in. She kept going back to the window. Maybe he would come right out again. He was with that big stupid Polack. She was getting angrier by the minute. More worried by the second.

She was a little woman. Spokes took after her in that. Short for his age. Helene had olive skin that looked tan even in winter. Her honey-brown hair lightened in the summer as her skin got darker until they were finally one color. "Stay out of the sun," her mother used to tell her, "it makes you look like a Puerto Rican." But she never listened to her mother. Spokes took after her in that, too.

Helene the rebel. What did it get her? Alone with a child, she felt old. She'd been little more than a child herself when she got married. Her mother told her she was too young, told her she shouldn't marry a traveling salesman—he's never home. But Helene was sold on him.

He died when Willy was three. Auto accident.

She still had more than a touch of the rebel in her. She was stubbornly independent. Wouldn't take a dime. It was her strength and it was her failing. It made it hard for anyone to get close. She was too busy, had to show them all.

Got herself a job at a neighborhood travel agency. A typical housewife job. Nothing particularly rebellious in that—think again. Leave it to Helene to start her own importing business.

She always loved jewelry. Lots of jewelry. So while on a "fam trip"—industry jargon for a discount junket provided by a tour company to familiarize travel agents with their packages—she just couldn't help herself; she brought back about a dozen too many silver bracelets from Mexico. Upon realizing her extravagance, she invited some neighborhood women over for coffee and cake. It didn't take long for them to get around to admiring Helene's new jewelry. Before the last of the Sara Lee was gone, she'd sold all twelve—and at a handsome profit, too. And so the Bracelet Lady came into being. She became a walking advertisement, a dozen bracelets on each wrist. It was the Tupperware tactic applied to the jewelry business. And business was good. Helene Freeman was finally getting somewhere, making a world for herself.

She jingle-jangled out of the apartment building intent on protecting her world. As she crossed Ralph Avenue, the screeching of brakes and the honking of horns heralded her coming.

Sitting in the branches of the old willow, carving his initials with a pocketknife, a boy with a pixie face perked up at the sight of Mrs. Freeman headed his way. He folded the blade and stood up. Sure enough, she was headed straight for the entrance. He turned and cupping his hand to the side of his mouth he hollered, "Spokes's mother's coming."

The cry was relayed through the lots like a native telegraph in a primitive jungle—"Spokes's mother's coming"—from the boy in the tree to another sitting on the concrete slab; to a little blonde boy who was hidden in the weeds, feeling up Angela Gerloven; to a couple of little savages busy stripping a ditched stolen car. From the roof of the car, the news passed to the outpost in the sycamore. And by the time Spokes' mom was making her way past the boulders at the entrance, the lookout sitting atop the lean-to lifted the hanging piece of carpet that served as a door. His upside down face turned red and shouted, "Spokes's mother's coming."

Inside the clubhouse, Spokes couldn't hear him. He was in another world. He didn't feel his body. He was feeling his spirit being stretched, drawn up to a canopy of vaulting trees. Incredibly tall thin trees with sparse green leaves bending to greet him, lifting him up toward a light. He could hear the voices of his ancestors calling to him to come. Beyond the treetops, a brilliant light, but no glare. He could look right into it. The air felt strangely still and at the same time charged with electricity. A voice. From the light. From everywhere. It was no language he'd ever heard. The words, if that's what they were, dragged out as if in slow motion. They went right through him, wrapped around the core of his soul, taking measure of his...

Shaking was happening. Munchik had him by the shoulder, attempting to jostle him out of the bag. Spokes mumbled something angry and incoherent, then put his mouth and nose back in the bag. Munchik pulled back his fist and socked Spokes in the arm. Hard. If he weren't so high he would have cried out, but he just lowered the bag and turned to face Munch. Eyeball to eyeball, Munch looked right at him and said, "Your mother."

There was a split-second pause as Spokes' face registered. Then, suddenly, he threw a hard right hand into Munchik's shoulder, answering back, "Your mother!"

Again, a split-second pause. This time as Munchik sat there looking confused and hurt. He didn't always look hurt. Then he hit Spokes again. "Your mother."

"Your mother."

"Your mother."

"Your mother."

It was one of the worst things someone could say to you. They traded punches and the fighting quickly escalated until they came tumbling out of the lean-to kicking and gouging and punching. There they were, rolling on the ground, dust flying, limbs flailing, when all of a sudden, like a freeze frame, they stopped. Spokes' mother was standing right there in front of them.

Spokes looked at her. Horror and glue stuck to his face. Now he had really gone and done it. He'd never be able to face her again. There was nothing he could say. It would take a whole bottle of mouthwash to cover the smell.

He ran.

"William, get back here."

He was in big trouble now. Whenever she called him *William*, it meant he was in trouble. If she called him Will or Willy, it probably meant that she needed him to go to the store for something. If she called him Billy, that meant she had cookies and milk on the table. But if she called him *William*....

He didn't look back. He made like he didn't hear and just kept on going.

As he went over the hill by where the path leads down to the junkyards, he twisted his ankle and fell. The anesthetic effect of the glue was wearing off and he rocked back and forth on the ground holding his ankle. He knew it—God was punishing him. He got back to his feet and hobbled as fast as he could, out of the lots.

* * * * *

Come evening in the projects in the summer, neighbors sat out on the benches in front of the buildings. It usually broke up about ten-thirty or eleven, a little later on the weekends.

It was twelve-thirty when Helene finally got up from the bench. It was beginning to turn a little chilly. She went slowly up the steps to the building. She kept thinking that he didn't even have a jacket or a sweater with him.

~~~

Chapter 7

There is a time for departure even when there's no certain place to go.

—*Tennessee Williams*

Spokes left the lots not knowing where he was going. All he knew was that he couldn't go home. He walked and walked and wound up at *the Junction*—where Flatbush and Church Avenues come together, by the subway station at the end of the line.

The glue on his face had hardened like bubble gum. Looking in the mirror of a parked car and spitting on his fingers, he tried to peel it off as best he could.

At a newsstand, he was looking through a magazine when he heard the train rumble in. He put the magazine back, deftly palmed a pack of gum off the counter, and ran down the stairs— as if he didn't want to miss his train. ...Clean as a whistle.

Once below, what do you know—the teller wasn't in the token booth. Must've stepped out for a moment. No transit police in sight. *Might as well*—he vaulted the turnstile. Kept going. Onto the train. The doors closed behind him.

He sat down. The car was practically empty. As it pulled out of the station he folded a stick of spearmint into his mouth.

Funny, but for someone who'd lived his whole life in Brooklyn, Spokes hardly ever went to Manhattan....

Nighttime was underway as he came up out of the subway, the stairs opening into an alcove under a bank building along Sixth Avenue. This was a different nighttime than the nighttime in Brooklyn. It might be the same moon in the same sky, but it was a different nighttime. He sat on the edge of the banister that wound down the stairwell—his feet were tired—and he watched the street. It was lined with vendors, craftspeople, artists. A stream of foot traffic went steadily by.

...As the gray sky gradually took on deepening shades of navy, the sidewalk show went into full swing. Like a carnival. The spectators were the spectacle. Spokes waded out into the din. And soon... he was swept up in it, pulled along from sideshow to sideshow. A portrait artist was busy at work—pen and ink caricatures. There was a man making beautiful rings out of old spoons. A juggler on a unicycle drew a big crowd. A man with a bunch of balloons and a helium tank stood in the gutter and shouted at cars. A tenor saxophonist held sway near the corner.

Turning the corner, Spokes found himself on a narrow side street where people with guitar cases lined up under a tattered awning at the entrance to a seedy little club—Star City. He decided to walk over to get a closer look. Along the side of the building there were pictures of famous singers and comedians. Under each celebrity was their name with the inscription: First N.Y.C. Appearance. And under that, the date. These were really big stars!

"Hey, the line starts back there." Some prick was worried that Spokes was trying to cut in line.

Spokes ignored him.

Someone else was watching him: a dark black girl with a shiny red bandana on her head and gold loop earrings, tight jeans and high heels. She was leaning on a cardboard guitar case at the end of the line. He didn't look away. Neither did she. She covered the flash of her pearly whites with her hand. He smiled back and walked over.

"Hi... whatcha doin'?" He introduced himself.

Her name was Pat and she was waiting for a number.

Tuesday night was showcase night at Star City. Performers got there when the doors opened so they could pick a number. The number was the order, when you got to go on. Singers got to do three songs; comics, fifteen minutes. If your number was higher than 25, there was no point hanging around. You'd end up playing to an empty house. The best numbers were between 12 and 20. That usually fell between ten o'clock and twelve.

Suddenly the doors opened and everyone filed in. It was dark inside. They were getting ready, taking chairs down off tables. To the left was the bar; to the right, a few booths. Behind the front room was a larger room filled with tables, and against the wall on the right, the stage.

Mark, the MC, held the hat that held the numbers. Pat held her breath and drew—number 19. Mark wrote down her name— Patricia Reed, number 19. She was happy about that.

...In the meantime, Pat decided to head over to Bleecker Street.

Willy decided to tag along. She seemed happy about that, too.

She had a long stride for a little girl. As they maneuvered along the crowded sidewalks, every few feet someone else would call out: "Hi, Pat." "What's happening, Pat?" "Looking good, Pat."

She seemed to know just about everyone. Kinda like Spokes in the projects, 'cept this was Greenwich Village.

"Gee, you sure know a lot of people." Willy was obviously impressed.

"Yeah, ' guess I do." She took it in stride.

She was the most natural person in the world. He was sure of it.

They stopped in front of a doorway, away from any shops, and not directly below any windows. Pat told him this was a good spot. She'd been working it for months. People on the block had grown accustomed to seeing her there.

She took out her guitar, strapped it on, and started to play. Her fingers gently shaped the sound and she smiled. And when she began to sing, it was really remarkable. Somehow her voice, her sweet clear voice, was able to penetrate the thick formless hum of the street. She wasn't loud. Just honest. Her voice was like a bell on a buoy; her smile, a beacon. Such a small voice touching at the heart of such a big city. Spokes recognized at once—it was magic.

People slowed as they walked past. They threw coins and bills into the cardboard case. And each time, Pat would say thanks. In the middle of a verse, with a smile and a nod, or a quick *Thank you* squeezed in—without losing a beat.

Most people, even those who gave, kept walking.

But little by little, a few stopped to listen, and soon a small crowd formed. She was as wonderful to look at as she was to listen to. Spokes watched her and he watched the reaction to her. Okay—so the audience wasn't as taken with her as he was. Still, most people stayed till the end of a song, long enough to offer some applause, then leave.

But this one group—two girls, a guy, and a child—they didn't leave. They stood off to the side, applauding boisterously and carrying on. Pat didn't pay any attention to them until after about the third song. While she fixed the capo to the neck of the guitar, she leaned over and said, "Hey, what's a matter with you guys? Can't you see I'm working? Do I go to McDonald's and bother you while you're working...?

"Willy, I want you to meet some friends of mine." First she introduced Willy to the short Irish-looking girl. "This is Pat, also."

She shook his hand. "Hi, Willy. You can call me Patty. Some people call us White Pat and Black Pat."

Next, Black Pat introduced him to Gypsy. He started to offer his hand, then settled for a smile. She had her hands full— her little boy, Jason, clung to her. She was chubby and looked very comfortable to cling to.

And the last-but-not-least belonged to Chance Langston. He shook Willy's hand like it was a spigot on a country well.

So these were Pat's friends. Not the same way half the people on the street were Pat's friends. These were her good friends.

Pat went back to singing. Patty sidled up to the new kid on the block. She was being very obvious, looking him over. She said to him, "Pat sang on tv once, on 'Showtime at the Apollo'. Did you know that?"

"No, I didn't..."

Pat looked over at them; her guitar playing became a tad more forceful. She stopped singing long enough to interrupt their conversation. "Down girl, I found him first."

"Well, pardon me," White Pat feigned indignant.

It was just good-natured kidding, but Willy never felt so flattered. He was having a great time.

White Pat moved over one, and Chance filled in. Chance was the type of guy who would tell his life story to a stranger he just met in a Laundromat. He was a comic. His idol was Andy Kaufman, who played Latke on "Taxi." Chance modeled himself after Andy Kaufman; he knew all his routines. Andy Kaufman—that was Chance's absolute favorite subject. And when he was talking, which was most of the time, he had an intensity bordering on hysteria. He had long stringy brown hair and the remnants of acne. He was from somewhere in the Midwest, Minnesota or Michigan—it was all the same to Spokes. Immediately upon graduating high school he came to New York to break into show business. He'd been here a year. If he was getting discouraged, it didn't show.

He decided to try out a new joke on the new guy: There's this man and his wife and they're driving down the highway when they get pulled over for speeding by the Highway Patrol. The cop says to the man, "Do you know you were going 80 miles an hour?" "I was not!" says the man. "You can't tell me you weren't speeding. I was driving right behind you for the past quarter mile," says the cop. "I clocked you on the radar gun." "I don't care what you or your radar says, I wasn't speeding." Meanwhile the cop's writing out a ticket and he hands it to the man and says, "Just sign here." "I ain't signing nothing," says the man, "because I wasn't speeding!" Now the cop turns to the man's wife and says, "Is he always this argumentative?" "No," says the man's wife, "only when he's drunk."

Willy smiled.

Chance laughed like a wild man. "Only when he's drunk." His mannerisms were so exaggerated; he was definitely funnier than his jokes, in an awkward kind of way.

Willy couldn't help but like him.

By the time they headed back to Star City, Willy was feeling right at home with his newfound friends. Black Pat walked on his left. She put her arm around his waist. So he put his arm around her shoulders. White Pat snuggled up on his right, lifting his other arm and putting it on her shoulder. They all smiled and laughed. If his friends from the park could only see him now—

walking around Greenwich Village, a girl on each arm.

But as he approached Star City, Willy started to worry. *What if I get asked for proof of age?* He had a phony ID on him, but it looked phony. What if he got caught? He didn't want Pat, either Pat, to know how old he was. They were at least 18, maybe even 19. *What if they think I'm too young?*

Showcase night was in full swing at the Star. Laughter followed by applause erupted from the back as they walked in. The doorman was sitting on a stool just inside the entrance. A hand lettered piece of cardboard was Scotch taped to the wall: $2 Cover.

"Hey, Jay, what do you say?" Black Pat stopped to give the tall chubby doorman a kiss on his unshaven cheek.

"There's supposed to be A&R from Polydor down front. Came here to hear this group, New Huevos Rancheros—Mexican punk rock. ...What's next?"

"Thanks, Jay."

Evidently the sign didn't apply to them. They breezed right in and found seats along the back wall. Gray duct tape crisscrossed the torn padding on the benches in their booth.

"Now behave yourselves. I'll be right back," Black Pat admonished as she got up. She left and went over to one of the tables near the stage where Mark, the MC, was sitting. He was with one of the most beautiful girls Willy had ever seen.

"Who is that?" he asked White Pat.

"That's Mark. He's the MC."

"No, not the guy. The—"

69

"Oh, that's Lucrecia.... They're made for each other. He's an asshole and she's a butt-plug." Patty lowered her voice and put her hand in front of her mouth. "She used to go with Chance until a few days ago. She dumped him. Best thing that could've happened to him. But don't tell him that. He's sick over her... but she's not worth it."

Willy looked closer at Patty's face. There was more than a little disaffection registered there. She wasn't very pretty. Sexy maybe. But jealousy and resentment made her look ugly. She must have known. Because as she noticed Willy looking at her, the rancor melted and a warm smile rushed in to take its place.

"I'm next," Black Pat announced as she sat back down next to Willy. "They're up to number 18."

A waitress came around. Pat waved her on, but Gypsy ordered a glass of sherry. Jason had curled up on the seat and was fast asleep. Which got Willy thinking, *Where am I going to sleep the night?*

"Where do you girls live...? I mean, do you live in the Village?" he asked, trying to feel out the subject.

Chance butted in, saying, "Cockroach Art."

It didn't seem like an answer. Willy was beginning to suspect that Chance wasn't just acting loony.

White Pat said, "He said 'girls.' Are you a girl?"

"Yeah, are you a girl?" Black Pat echoed. "...Maybe there's something you've been holding out on us?"

"Oh, well, you found me out. I'm really a dyke masquerading as a guy to get into your pants. Anything to get a little black and white Pat-Pat puss."

"Chance, you're really a jerk, masquerading as a person."

"What's he talking about? Cockroach Art?" Willy wanted to know.

"You mean you've never heard of the world famous Cockroach Art?" Chance said.

"Don't worry, Willy, neither has anybody else. You'll see. We'll go there later," Black Pat assured him.

The singer on the stage had just finished a sappy love song. It had to be an original—it was too bad to be anything but.... Mark, the MC, took the mic to introduce the next act.

Pat had her guitar out.

Willy didn't know Pat well enough to notice, but she was more anxious than usual. She'd spotted the A&R reps from the record label, two guys and a girl, seated to the right of the stage, looking way too fashionable for Star City.

Mark's voice, deep and affected: "And now folks, I want you to give a special Star City welcome to this next act. I know you're going to enjoy... New Huevos Rancheros."

Pat cursed under her breath, "That fuck! He did that on purpose."

Willy whispered to Chance, "Hey, what's going on? I thought Pat was next?"

"Yeah, but sometimes for record company people they bump the order. Mark's been doing it a lot lately. Kiss ass yuppie bastard."

The group on the stage glared at the audience as they spit,

twanged, and yodeled their way through a country western punk rock song. Slam dance do-si-do—they were so bad, they were amusing.

...To everyone but Pat.

Their set dragged on past the usual three songs. Some folks in the audience couldn't take it anymore. A few tables emptied.

"These guys are going to clear the room," Pat griped.

She still had hopes of getting on while the talent scouts were there.

But then, after New Huevos, Mark took the mic and started doing his standup.

"That prick!" She said it loudly. Practically everyone heard.

Chance explained to Willy, "Being the MC has perks. All night long he gets to work in a few jokes between acts and he also gets to pick his spot."

Halfway though his routine, the A&R people got up to go.

"Good! They're being rude to you," Pat was thinking out loud.

"The beautiful people" waved *bye-bye* to Mark as they made their way out.

From the stage he thanked them for stopping by—like they were old friends. Like he understood that they had to leave just then and it was fine with him.

Pat said to the others, "Come on. Let's get the fuck out of here."

"But you're on next. Aren't you—"

"I don't feel like singing.... Come on, Willy, don't you want to come with me?"

So they piled out of Star City.

Jay the doorman said goodnight. Pat didn't bother to say goodnight back. Willy just shrugged. Heck, it wasn't his fault.

Back on the street the 'BS' faded fast. It was a beautiful night. It had cooled down quite a bit. A little chilly even. The sidewalks were still filled with people as they made their way back toward Bleecker.

"So, where we going?" Willy asked.

"You'll see," White Pat answered.

They padded around a few corners, down a few side streets, through a small parking lot filled with bakery trucks, through a hole in a fence, to a chained and padlocked back door of an abandoned industrial building.

"Wow! What is this place?" Willy stopped in his tracks.

"Just follow us," Gypsy said as she passed a sleeping Jason through to Chance, through the crack of the open door, courtesy of slack in the chain. She squeezed in after. Willy hesitated, then followed.

Once inside he had to stop again to adjust his vision to the low light. There didn't seem to be any windows and there were only two small points of light—one red bulb over the exit behind him and another over a door at the far end of the corridor.

The others kept walking. Through it all Jason was still sleeping in his mother's arms. As she passed through another door, she turned: "Aren't you coming?"

Willy ran to catch up, rejoining them in what appeared to be a small lobby.

All of a sudden he became aware he was running too fast. The soles of his shoes weren't gripping on the smooth terrazzo floor. Willy went sliding—

Then out of the blue, without notice or provocation, Chance hit him square in the chest. The punch, combined with the speed Willy was moving, was enough to floor him.

He got up quickly, fighting mad. "I don't know what the fuck's going on, but—"

Pat stepped in. "He saved your ass, that's what."

"I'm sorry, Willy," Chance was saying. "I didn't mean to... not that hard. Really, I'm sorry..."

Willy lowered his fists.

A few feet in front of him, alongside where the others were standing, was an open elevator shaft. The relic of a knee-high safety gate was pulled closed across the threshold. Not much safety there.

Willy was taken aback by just how close he had come.... "Geez, I'm the one that's sorry. Pat's right! Chance, you saved my ass."

Just then the pulleys and cables came to life and the elevator rattled down and jerked to a stop—about a foot above floor level. Pat stepped over the broken gate, up and in. The others did likewise. Willy hesitated, then he too got in.

"This thing really works!?" Willy's words started as a comment, but ended as more of a question.

"I sure hope so!" Gypsy wasn't overly reassuring.

Again the mechanism whirred into action. It was a freight

elevator with heavy quilted pads against two walls. The back wall was open, just like the front. A single white light on each landing illuminated the rough-surfaced concrete wall passing their slow ascent. Willy was still facing forward when they came to an abrupt halt. At first he thought they'd stopped between floors. All he saw was a wall in front of him,. The landing was opposite from where they entered. Willy was facing the wrong way. Chance turned him around. They stepped up and out of the elevator—this time it stopped about a foot short.

"*Tah dah!*... Chance announced, "Welcome to Cockroach Art, home of the soon to be rich and famous."

They were standing on the fifth floor in a tremendous loft space. The room was faintly lit by more of those red bulbs; furnished in urban nonconformity: couches, beach chairs, a picnic table, a bar with bar stools, mattresses, a refrigerator, even a small tv. The windows were partially covered by hanging sheets.

"Wow! This place is great!"

"You want a cold one?" White Pat, standing at the open frig, tossed him a can of beer.

Black Pat switched on the tv.

Willy marveled, "Everything works! It's like a real home."

~~~

Chapter 8

It takes all the fun out of a bracelet if you have to buy it yourself.

—*Peggy Joyce*

Helene Freeman had put her life on hold. She had to in order to raise Willy. At least that was the way she thought. She felt more comfortable that way. She was more modern in her attitudes than her mother, but she still had old-fashioned ideas when it came to the sanctity of the home and the family.

From the outside looking in, her life may have looked exciting, especially to the other women in the projects. Helene went on her *fam* trips and sold her jewelry. But the truth was that without Willy there, the loneliness rushed in on her like a chill. Her world was no bigger than a boy. She hadn't let a man in her life since Willy's dad died. Not that she hadn't attracted her share over the years. She was still pretty. But she told herself that she wasn't interested just now, and the inquiries grew few and far between. But it was okay because Willy needed her. It hadn't occurred to her that maybe she was the one that needed.

"He'll be back," her mother told her. "Remember the time you ran away from home. It's part of growing up. Willy's a good boy. Better at taking care of himself than most."

Mothers didn't know everything. Kids were different these days. There were more drugs and more crazies on the streets. Helene had to do something. She called around to the homes of some of Willy's friends. The other parents, most of whom she knew, offered their concern and agreed to contact her if they heard anything.

...Later that day, one of them called back.

What she had to say came as a surprise. The woman had learned from her son that Willy was hiding from an older boy named Rosey—that was all she knew. She hoped it might be of some help. Helene distractedly thanked her as she hung up. If this was true, then Willy's not being home wasn't her fault; it wasn't about what happened in the lots. There was something else going on here, something that she didn't understand.

What to do next?

The police said they couldn't do anything until after he'd been reported missing for 48 hours, and even then... they didn't sound encouraging. Runaways weren't exactly a top priority.

It was no use. She couldn't think clearly anymore. It was late in the afternoon when she decided to take a walk.

She wasn't sure why she walked in that particular direction. Maybe it was subconscious, maybe it was pure coincidence. But she found herself in front of the Regent Supper Club, a small lounge adjacent to a large catering hall. They were both owned by the same family: the Tjoepani's. She'd been there once before. About a year ago. A neighbor's kid got *bar mitzvah'd*. It was a very beautiful affair. Helene wasn't the type to go into bars. But then, this really wasn't a bar. It was a *supper club*, much more elegant. She rarely took a drink—didn't keep liquor in the house—but she suddenly felt like one. She also felt a little funny going inside. She wasn't dressed properly. Besides, it was probably too early.

She went in.

There were no windows. Sconces streaked light onto the walls. It felt like nighttime. A musician was setting up equipment on the small stage in the corner. A bartender was leaning on his elbow, studying a racing form. She was the only customer.

She sat at a table. She sat and she sat.

She looked around for a waitress—no waitress. The bartender glanced up but then went back to the ponies. She fidgeted in her purse, took out a five dollar bill, and placed it on the table.

She was about to get up and leave when she saw him. She hadn't noticed him there when she first walked in. And she didn't see him come in, but he was suddenly there. He crossed the floor to the bartender. He was wearing a tuxedo. It fit beautifully, but seemed to pull slightly across the back. He was too muscular for formal wear. He looked the same as he did when they'd met. She'd forgotten all about him, or had she?

The bartender snapped to attention, nodding and saying, "Yes, sir. Right away, sir." He came out from behind the bar; in a flash he was at her table. She ordered a slo3 gin fizz. He lit her cigarette, then hurried back with her cocktail. When she tried to pay, he told her, "Please accept it, compliments of the house."

She looked over at the man in the tuxedo. He was still standing there, alongside the bar. He nodded a hello and smiled.

"Please thank Mr. Malfieri for me," she told the bartender.

Mr. Malfieri—she had opened her mouth and it rolled off her tongue. She was surprised at herself for remembering his name—Jimmy Malfieri. He had been very nice to her at Mrs. Bromberg's son's bar mitzvah. At the end of the evening, when one of the other women at her table got to take home the centerpiece, he must have seen her disappointment because he went in the back and returned with an absolutely gorgeous bouquet—just for her. But then Helene thought, *That's his job. He's supposed to see that the guests are happy. It was just part of his job.*

"Hello, Mrs. Freeman, so nice to see you again." He was standing there at her table offering his hand.

"Thank you.... Would you care to join me?"

Again he smiled.

"...And please, call me Helene."

They made small talk. He admired her bracelets. She told him about her jewelry business. He seemed genuinely interested. She was flattered by the attention, truly glad for the company. He was so handsome. Maybe *handsome* wasn't the right word. No matter, she felt good sitting with him. It had been so long since anyone had...

Suddenly there was a terrible guilt—that she could allow herself any good feelings at a time like this, when she didn't even know where her baby was. How could she?

Confusion and panic commandeered her eyes. The tears just

burst out.

"Ah, hey, there now." He was caught totally off guard. He moved a little closer, putting his hand on her shoulder, to comfort her.

She buried her face against his chest and sobbed.

She felt the hardness of a gun in a shoulder holster.

It took a while, but she regained her composure, pulling back and sitting up straight. Jimmy produced a handkerchief. She took it and blotted her eyes.

"I'm so embarrassed. I'm sorry. I'm not usually like this. Really, I—"

"Hey, it's okay. It's okay."

A waitress had arrived on the floor to start her shift. Jimmy raised his hand. She came right over.

"Bring the lady another drink."

"Yes, Mr. Malfieri." She took the empty glass and swiveled her hips to the bar and back.

After she'd put the fresh drink down, as she was walking away, Helene commented, "She's a very pretty girl."

"Yeah, she's alright."

When he spoke he didn't even glance at the waitress. He didn't take his eyes off Helene. A small smile staggered back to her face.

"There, now that's better." He took her hand. "Would it help to talk about it? If there's anything I can do...?"

"You've already been too kind. I hardly know you and here I am crying all over your beautiful tuxedo. ...No, really, I think I'd better be getting back."

"I assure you, I'm not being *too* kind. I like you. And as for you hardly knowing me, that's something we should work on. If you have to go, at least let me take you home?"

"No, that's very nice of you, but I'm sure you have more important things to do. I'll be just fine. Really. Thanks, but it's not necessary."

"Please. Believe me, I have nothing more important to do."

They looked into each other's eyes. Then, without another word, they got up and left.

~~~

Chapter 9

Serious sport has nothing to do with fair play. It is bound up with hatred, jealousy, boastfulness, disregard of all rules and sadistic pleasure...

—*George Orwell*

The park felt like spring. With the hot spell broken, cool breezes played on the air. Rosey was feeling like playing ball.

In high school he had been a serious ball player. He desperately needed to feel the distraction of those bygone days. A bunch of kids were playing stickball on the big asphalt diamond. A high chain link fence separated it from the handball courts on the far side; the park house and the benches, on the other side. Rosey walked around the fence and down the incline behind the backstop.

"Hey kid, lemme see that bat for a minute." Rosey squirted spit between his teeth.

The rules of stickball were general knowledge to all project residents. You didn't need a lot of players to have a game. Two would do, but four was better. You didn't use a glove, but it was helpful if you were playing catcher. But you didn't really need a catcher either. There was no running bases. You had one or two fielders. All you really needed was a pitcher. Spaulding was the ball of choice though most agreed the new Pency Pinky bounced higher. If a grounder got past you, it was a single. If a fly ball hit the bottom two rungs of the fence, you could catch it off the fence and it would be out. If it hit the third or top rung, or if you didn't catch it off the fence, it was a double. If it went over the fence and fell into the handball courts, it was a triple. And if it went over both fences and into the street, it was a home run.

The kid at bat was looking at a six to four lead—theirs, two outs, two men on base, one strike, two balls, and Rosey asking to see the bat for a minute. He looked to the pitcher, to the guys on his team. They all shrugged in acceptance. For a split second the batter appeared hesitant, even reluctant.

"Hey, kid, I'm not gonna eat it. I just want to see it for a minute, you understand?" Rosey snatched the stickball bat out of his hands. The kid didn't try to hold onto it. That would've been just plain stupid. Everyone in the park knew who Rosey was.

Rosey gripped the bat up high and took a few short warm-up swings. "Okay, go 'head. Pitch one."

The pitcher put one low and inside. Rosey swung, clipping the ball; it fouled back behind the plate.

He spit and pumped the stick for the next pitch.

Again, low and inside. This time he didn't swing. He caught the ball himself and tossed it back. "One and one. See if you can't put one over." He was calling his own pitches now. No one said a thing.

Rosey spit. The pitcher looked nervous. He threw a wild one, high and outside. It rattled the backstop and bounced away.

The catcher went after it. So did Rosey. As the catcher reached for the ball, Rosey pushed him aside. The kid fell, scraping his elbow. Rosey picked up the ball.

"Hey, Campy, get over here," he hollered.

Under a tree near the park house, Campy was sitting on the backrest of a bench reading the *Daily News*. He folded the paper, tucking it under his arm, and in his characteristic saunter, started toward the field.

"Sometime this year, Campy. Whadaya say?"

"Hold your horses. I'm coming."

"Here," Rosey tossed him the ball, "you need the exercise. Pitch a few."

"You know, these guys are in the middle of a game, Rosey. They might not appreciate you interrupting it like this." Campy bounced the ball.

"Sure they do... You," Rosey addressed the pitcher, "you appreciate it, don't you?" He didn't give the kid time to answer. What could he possibly say! "Go play right field. I'll hit a few out. You'll get some fielding practice."

Campy looked at the kid and shrugged. Not much he could do either. "Okay, just a couple," he said to Rosey.

Rosey stripped off his shirt, and tossed it behind the plate. Wearing a wife-beater t-shirt, he pumped the stickball bat a few times, then pointed toward the fence and across the avenue. Calling his shot. He tapped the end of the stick against the plate.

He was ready.

A small audience was gathering. A few kids on bikes stopped to admire Rosey's muscles. If he did knock one across the avenue, they would talk about it with reverence.

Not all those taking an interest were sports fans—or fans of Rosey's for that matter. Wolfee, who'd been standing by the basketball courts, ambled over, doing a slow bop down the first base line. The two Joeys decided to get out of the Caddy and stretch their legs. The kids on bikes made room for them behind the backstop.

Bonj spotted Wolfee; Wolfee spotted Bonj. But even before they actually saw each other, there was a ripple in the air. A danger signal. Like a kind of radar. For a second, Bonj thought Wolfee might bolt. LaPela put a hand on Bonj's shoulder. Wolfee couldn't hear him from where he was but he could tell, LaPela was telling Bonj that this wasn't the time or the place. LaPela himself didn't so much as acknowledge Wolfee's presence. Not that it mattered to Wolfee. He wasn't the least bit offended. He leaned back against the fence and eased himself down into a comfortable sitting position. He didn't take his eyes off Bonj. Like he was daring him—*come and get me*. Since Freddy's death, Wolfee was acting like he was tired all the time—tired of living.

Bonj looked away first.

LaPela was talking to him, cracking wise about a growing problem: the proliferation of sports amongst the nation's hard drug users. His humor was lost on Bonj. No matter, Rosey had heard him.

So all the players were there, and this crowd wasn't much for games. Rosey paid no attention to any of them. He was going to play stickball. He waited for the pitch.

Campy was clowning around on the mound. Finally he threw a fastball that rose slightly as it sailed over the plate.

"Steerrike one," the catcher hammed it up.

Rosey raised his eyebrows and spit between his teeth. He pumped the stick a few times and hit the end against the ground.

The second pitch was a carbon copy of the first, only this time Rosey swung. He smacked the ball out to center field. It was still climbing when it hit the third rung of the fence. A good shot. But not good enough for Rosey. He was intent on putting one out of the park.

"Okay, that was a warm up. Now I'm getting the feel." He obviously wasn't ready to give up the bat.

So Campy wound up and delivered another fastball. Rosey swung, only this time he didn't make solid contact. He sliced it. It popped up and went foul over the fence alongside the third base line. It dropped into the street, rolling to the curb on the other side. One of the little kids took off on his bike to retrieve it.

Before the kid could get to it, a man in a short leather jacket, dress slacks, and expensive shoes, bent to pick up the ball.

"Hey, mister, give it here."

The man called the kid over. He said something to the kid, and the kid pointed to home plate.

The man walked slowly up to the fence.

"Throw the ball over," Campy asked, "please."

The man didn't pay any attention to Campy. He held the ball in his hands making no motion at all to throw it.

Rosey's eyebrows twitched, followed by the squirt of spit, and without looking up at the man, he barked, "Throw the fucking ball over the fence."

"Your name Rosey?" the man spoke. He wasn't so much asking as serving notice.

Almost immediately Bonj recognized the well-dressed stranger.

"Hey, Joey, isn't that the guy ' works for your uncle?" Bonj said, like he was telling LaPela something he didn't already know.

"Shut up," LaPela told him, "I want to hear this."

Rosey sneered at the stranger. "What's it to you?" He strode to the fence with the stickball bat in his hand. When he got right up next to it, he whipped the bat at the man's face.

The fence rattled violently, taking the onlookers by surprise. Practically everyone recoiled with the suddenness of the strike— everyone except *the man*.

He didn't so much as flinch.

A long standstill held as the two sized each other up. It was hard to say just who was being protected by the intervening fence.

When they resumed talking, it was as if they had silently come to some sort of understanding.

Without speaking softly, the man spoke quietly so that none of those nearby could hear. "This has got to do with the little kid, William Freeman. I'm a friend of the family."

"I don't know no William Freeman," Rosey looked puzzled. "...Campy, you know a little kid named William Freeman?"

"You know Willy," Campy answered. "That's Spokes." He started to leave the pitcher's mound to join in the conversation. Rosey held up a hand. Campy got the message; he didn't come any closer.

"Okay, I know him. So what?"

"So there's a rumor you mean to hurt him."

"Nah, that ain't true. I just want to find the kid... to find out who put him up to it."

"Who put him up to what?"

"Nothing... it's not important. A practical joke—somebody put the kid up to a practical joke, is all. I'm not gonna hurt him. I don't go around pickin' on little kids."

"And you have no idea where he is?"

"No idea. God's honest truth."

"Okay... but you find him, you let me know. His mother's real worried. Ask for Jimmy Malfieri at the Regent Supper Club. I'll see that you're taken care of. ...And if you're lying to me and you hurt that kid... I'll see that you're taken care of."

Rosey thought about it for a minute, then raised his voice, "Don't fuckin' threaten me. Nobody fuckin' threatens me."

Jimmy took a step back from the fence and tossed the ball over, saying, "Be smart, tough guy, and play ball." He turned and walked back to his car.

Campy caught the ball. He looked at it and began to shake his head.

Rosey turned on him, "Now what the fuck's wrong with you?"

"Ball's cracked." Campy demonstrated, throwing the ball down. It didn't bounce back up. "Must've broke when you hit it."

"Fuck!" Rosey swung the stickball bat into the metal fence post, splintering the wood and sending the broken end flying off the handle.

As the two Joeys were walking away, LaPela was thinking aloud, "I don't think we're going to have to go to Uncle Tjoepani with this problem after all... least not directly."

~~~

Chapter 10

...talent instantly recognizes genius.

—*Sir Arthur Conan Doyle*

Willy soon learned that Chance Langston was the only full-time resident of Cockroach Art, or as he liked to put it—the curator. There were no paintings on the walls. No one ever needed to ask how the place got its name.

White Pat didn't stayed overnight. She lived nearby in the East Village. The same went for Gypsy and Jason. Black Pat lived uptown in Harlem with her mom and a younger brother. She was one tough cookie. But recently she'd had a bad experience going home late one night. She was attacked on the subway, and she was stabbed. As is often the case, the physical wounds healed first. She was still pretty freaked by the ordeal. So she'd been staying over at the Cockroach a lot lately rather than take the train back late at night.

...It was a Thursday night and not even Black Pat was there, just Chance and Willy. Outside a summertime thunderstorm was pounding the streets, had been for hours. Willy found a joint that someone lost behind the cushions of the couch and now he was combing the place hoping to find another. It was beginning to seem like the rain was never going to let up. He was getting antsy.

"Willy, relax. We're high and dry. What more do you want?"

"I want it to stop raining."

"It will. And as soon as it does we'll go out, and the streets will be clean, and the air will be clean, and we'll go to the Pizza Box. I got some money." Chance worked as a panhandler near the 8th Avenue subway. He was good at it—he had the look. "In the meantime... I'm supposed to go to The Improv tomorrow to do a guest spot and I've been working on a new routine. How's about if you have a seat and I do my act? Give me a chance to try it out in front of an audience."

"A captive audience, huh?"

"Okay, great! You sit right there. I'll go get my stuff."

Sometimes it was tough to get a word in edgewise with Chance.

"What kind of stuff?" Willy asked. "I thought you were a stand-up?"

"You'll see."

Chance hurried to the small storage room in the back of the loft. He opened the padlocked door and dragged out a small trunk. He pushed it to the middle of the room and, using another key, he unlocked it.

"Turn around. I'm not ready yet. It'll just take me a minute. And no peeking."

Willy did as he was asked, turning his back for a minute

while Chance made like a whirlwind, rearranging furniture.

"Hey, what the hell are you doing? renovating the place?"

"Okay, I'm ready. You can turn around now."

Chance was too much. He'd cleared the middle of the loft to form his stage. A lamp on the floor became a footlight shining up at him.

He began by turning the trunk around, 360 degrees, like a magician revealing that there was nothing up his sleeves: "It's show time!" He provided his own background music—"daa da da da dadaa da da da..." He flipped open the lid, with the back of the trunk toward his audience, pulled out a cassette player, and placed it on a chair directly behind him. He took a cassette out of his shirt pocket and put it into the tape player. The whole time he kept humming the cliché showbiz theme. Then, with a slow dramatic wave of his index finger, he pushed the play button. From out of the speaker—*daa da da da dadaa da da da...*—a tape of Chance humming the cliché showbiz theme. It picked up right where he left off. Chance thanked the imaginary crowd.

Willy found himself chuckling. But Chance was taking no chances—the tape also contained a laugh track.

"Good evening," he announced. "My name is Chance Langston and tonight it will be my pleasure to entertain you... with the art of ventriloquism. So without further ado, allow me to introduce my lovely assistant—Cherry Wood."

Willy applauded on cue like a good audience.

Chance stood there with his hand outstretched, pointing to the open trunk—like he expected Cherry to pop out all by herself. Again he said, "Cherry Wood."

This time the canned applause was peppered with snickering. After another awkward moment of Chance standing there expectantly, he finally walked to the trunk.

"Cherry Wood if she could—no seriously, if you've ever wondered why you don't see more women ventriloquist dummies, this is why! Too temperamental, difficult to work with!" Then, looking into the trunk he said, "It's show time, Cherry. People are waiting."

A husky but definitely feminine voice was clearly heard to say "Drop dead" just before the lid of the trunk was pulled shut.

The tape player bleated out a volley of canned laughter.

Undaunted, Chance plodded on. "Gee, folks, I'm sorry for this... Must be her time of the—"

Before he could finish, he met with a smattering of boos.

"—year. That's what I was going to say.... Her time of the year—autumn."

Now there were some hisses mixed in with the boos. He flinched at the jeering like he was dodging tomatoes.

"Cherry," he pleaded at the trunk. In a loud whisper he added, "I'm dying out here. You got to stop this. You're embarrassing me."

"I'm embarrassing you!" You could barely see Chance's lips move. "You got a lot of nerve. Night after night I have to sit on your lap while you 'goose' me, in front of all those people."

Willy was sitting up, taking notice. In addition to Cherry's voice being somewhat girlish, now that the trunk was closed, it had a muffled quality. One would swear it was coming from inside. This ventriloquism stuff interested him.

Chance played it straight-faced, quick to explain, "She's just kidding around. I don't goose her."

"You do too."

"I do not."

"You do too."

"I do not."

"Yeah, then tell me... what's my temperature?"

"Your temperature? How would I know your temperature?"

"If that's not a thermometer, then I'm being goosed."

Canned laughter.

"I am not goosing you," Chance insisted. The way Chance said *goose*... it was funny. Willy smiled, even laughed a little.

"It's not a thermometer? and it's not your finger goosing me...?"

"No!"

"Does your girlfriend call you *Pee Wee?*"

More canned laughter.

Chance actually blushed. "Let's not get personal, Cherry, okay?"

"Sounds good to me. Just keep your hands in plain view."

"Now you know I have to have my hand behind your back in order to operate your controls. You're just a dummy...."

"I see..." She didn't sound convinced. "Knock knock."

"Excuse me, but what did you say?"

"You heard me. I said *'Knock knock'*."

Cautiously, Chance replied, "Who's there?"

"Lois."

"Lois who?"

"Lowest form of human life—that's what you are!"

The laugh track hit right on cue. Chance had to have put a lot of rehearsing into this. His acting was pretty good, too. He was very convincing at looking surprised.

"That's it, I've had it with you. I take you out of the gutter, give you a good job, and this is the thanks I get." Chance was frantic. He rushed around in a panic—without hardly moving from his spot. Suddenly, he produced a saw. A small handsaw.

Oohs, *aahs*, and gasps filtered off the prerecorded response.

Chance grinned like Jack Nicholson. He reached into his coat pocket and came out with the key to the trunk. Then, with all the melodrama of Snidely Whiplash, he locked the trunk.

Having done that, he addressed his imaginary standing-room-only crowd: "Ladies and gentlemen, I am sorry to announce that due to technical difficulties beyond our control... Cherry Wood, the star of our show, will be... unable to go on with tonight's performance."

A knocking started coming from inside the trunk. Cherry could be heard saying "Chance, what are you doing? Don't do anything you'll be sorry about later."

The music stopped.

Chance definitely had a gleam in his eye. He took a moment to make believe the saw was a violin playing a sad refrain. Then, standing poised over the trunk, saw at the ready, he said, "Do you have any last words?"

The muffled voice from within the trunk sounded frightened as she said, "Knock knock."

"What's that you said?"

In a gruff tone, "You heard me. *Knock knock.*"

Once again, cautiously, Chance responded, "Who's there?"

"Diane."

"Diane who?"

"Die and go to hell, you bastard."

Cherry pealed with laughter. The make-believe audience laughed. The footlight clicked off. The sound of sawing wood filled the room. And soon the sound of muffled screams could be heard above the sawing.

The lights came back on. The tape recorder issued a tumultuous ovation. ...That was it. The end.

Willy wasn't sure what to make of it. What a strange ending! He applauded. What else could he do?

Once the furniture was put back where it belonged, Chance wanted to know, "Well, what did you think?"

"Hey, I liked it. You actually manage to do a ventriloquist act without a dummy. That's unique. Very clever. ...And you're pretty good at that ventriloquist stuff. I couldn't hardly see your lips moving at all."

Chance smiled deviously. "That's the clever part. I don't really do ventriloquism. I tried to learn it once, but that stuff's too hard. Cherry's voice is on tape. I have a second tape recorder inside the trunk. I just move my lips a little to make you think that it's me trying to make you think it's not me. It's the old double fake, get it?"

"So who's doing Cherry's voice?"

"That's Lucrecia. I had her make the tape for me a couple weeks ago, when we were still going out. I could never do that good an impersonation of a woman's voice."

"I can," Willy said without hesitation, then proceeded to demonstrate: "Knock knock. Chance you are the lowest form of human life."

Chance sat up straight, astounded by what he'd just heard. "How'd you do that?"

"How'd you do that?" Willy repeated. Only it wasn't Willy. It was Cherry Wood. It was Lucrecia's voice.

Chance moved his head as in a double-take. "Gee, that grass must have been stronger than I thought."

With his own Brooklyn accent, in his own adolescent voice, Willy said, "You can say that again." And then, with the smoothness of a race car driver shifting gears, he switched voices and was again Lucrecia as he said, "Gee, that grass must have been stronger than I thought."

"Holy shit! Where'd you learn to do that?" Chance wanted to know.

"Holy shit! Where'd you learn to—"

Chance put his hand over Willy's mouth. "Now stop... for a minute." Chance slowly removed his hand from Willy's mouth. Willy stayed still. He didn't say anything, his eyes staring out from behind the glaze. That weed really was stronger than they'd thought. He listened in the stillness—the sound of the rain in the background was gone. The munchies had set in. In his own hungry little voice he said, "It's time for pizza."

...So they went to the Pizza Box on Bleecker. As promised, Chance bought. And as they stuffed their faces, Chance continued to marvel at Willy's facility with voices. Where did he learn? How long has he had the ability? Could he do any impersonations of famous people?

Willy didn't really know. He'd never tried to imitate anybody except the guys from the park. He told Chance about how he'd played a joke on this guy by calling the "Dr. Leslie Gift Show" and making believe that he was that guy. He didn't go into too much detail about the incident, but Chance got the idea.

"Some of the guys in my neighborhood got real distinct ways a' talkin'," Willy explained, "so it's real easy to make fun a' them. That's what makes it easy, if the guy's voice got some special features. Take Pat, for example. Black Pat, she got this high voice that's real soft when she talks. She's always saying stuff like 'Willy, I be wanting to kiss you.'" It sounded like Pat was sitting right there. "And when she sings, you can't believe that sound comes from her." And then Willy actually demonstrated a few bars of Pat singing.

The pizza man turned to see where it was coming from.

"That's great! You got her down pat—no pun intended." Chance laughed his geeky laugh, impressed with himself—but not nearly so much as he was with Willy. "No, seriously, this is amazing. You can do singing voices, too. It's just amazing."

98

Chance went on and on, making a really big deal out of it. He said that Willy had a talent to be envied. He went so far as to say it was a gift—to be revered.

Willy considered what Chance was saying. Up until that instant he hadn't given it much thought. He hadn't perceived it as being of any great importance. But maybe Chance was right; after all, Chance was a smart fellow.

Chance was especially smart where Chance was concerned. And later, back at the Cockroach, when he had sufficiently recovered from being awestruck, he began to formulate a practical and immediate use for his discovery. It must have been one in the morning when he got Willy out of bed.

"Willy, I been thinking. Something you said, about calling the "Dr. Leslie Gift Show" and impersonating someone else's voice on the phone. I want you to do me a favor. What do you say? Will you do me a favor?"

"I don't know," Willy said sleepily. "You haven't told me what it is you want me to do."

"I want you to call Mark the asshole, the MC. Only I want you to call as Lucrecia. I know you can do it. I heard you do her voice; it was perfect."

"What do you want me to say to him?"

"I don't care, as long as you're horrible to him. You have to make it so he never wants to speak to her again. Say anything. Just be real mean."

"What if he likes it when she's mean? Some guys are like that. What then? You ever think of that?"

"Tell him he's just too stupid to be your boyfriend, that he smells bad, that he's a momma's boy—the guy still lives with his mother, can you imagine? Tell him you've decided you're going back to Chance."

"Yup... that ought to do it. I guess we got to do this now, huh...? Okay, what's his number?"

As they walked to a phone booth, Chance replayed the tape of Lucrecia's voice—to refresh Willy's memory. Willy decided it would work better if he pretended to be a little drunk.

The deception went off like a charm. Mark's mother answered the phone. She was not at all pleased at her son getting a call from such a rude, intoxicated young lady so late at night. Lucrecia had once told Chance how Mark and his mother were always fighting. Well after Willy's—or rather Lucrecia's—conversation with the old lady, they'd have something to fight about. And by the time Willy got done with Mark, he wasn't going to want to talk to Lucrecia ever again.

...Willy hung up the phone.

Chance was standing outside the phone booth jumping up and down. He was exhilarated. A crazy mix of revenge attained and hope regained—it was just what he needed.

"I owe you for this, Willy. That was great. Just great!"

"Listen, you got any more change? I gotta make a personal call."

"Sure. Here." Chance fished out a handful of coins and gave them to Willy. "Will that be enough?"

"Yeah, more than enough.... I'll only be a minute." Willy

closed the door.

"Take your time," Chance hollered. "I'm going to head over to the Kettle. I'll meet you there." He knocked on the side of the booth. "Great. Just great!"

Willy nodded, and Chance walked away, down the street to his favorite bar and grill.

Willy stared at the phone for a while. 251-5716—he could hear it ring. His pulse pounded in his ears. The other end picked up.

"Hello, Mom. It's me, Willy."

"Oh, thank God. Willy, where are you? I've been worried sick. Come home right this minute, you hear. Everything's going to be alright. Just come home."

"I'm okay, Ma. I just wanted you to know I'm okay. That's all."

"Where are you? I'll come get you. Just tell me where you are?"

"I don't need you to come get me. I'm fine. Really. I'm staying with some friends in the Village.

"The Village? You're in Greenwich Village? It's filled with creeps and homosexuals. I want you to come home right now."

"Is it him?" Jimmy whispered. The call had awakened him and he rolled over and saw Helene sitting up in bed.

She cupped her hand over the phone. "He's alright. He's in the Village."

"Mom, who are you talking to?" Willy asked.

Now it was Helene's turn to feel like the child caught

misbehaving. And for a moment they reversed roles. Suddenly she was the one who had some explaining to do. She wasn't at all sure how to handle this situation. This was all so totally new to her.

"Ma, I asked you, Who are you taking to?"

"A friend, dear. Your mother has... a friend. A very nice gentleman, Mr. Malfieri... Jimmy. He stopped by to visit with me. In fact, I've been telling him all about you and he'd like very much to meet you."

"Oh... I see. I'm sorry... I'm calling at a bad time. It's so late... and you have company."

"William... you don't know how upset I've been—not knowing if you were alive or dead."

"Yeah, I can tell, you're beside yourself. Well maybe not beside yourself, but beside somebody."

"William, stop it! I'm your mother. And I'm telling you to come home."

"I gotta go. I just wanted you to know that I'm alright. That's all. Ma... I gotta go. I'll call you later. Bye... bye, Ma."

Over her protests and her pleas, William hung up the receiver.

He started to walk away, down the street, and the phone rang. That would be the operator, a programmed voice asking that he *Please deposit another thirty-five cents, please...*

"Fuck you!" he yelled back, and walked away faster.

~~~

Chapter 11

To be thrown upon one's own resources, is to be cast into the very lap of fortune; for our faculties then undergo a development and display an energy of which they were previously unsusceptible.

—Benjamin Franklin

Summer in the city was turning out to be a gas. This living on your own wasn't so tough—at least that was Willy's initial assessment. The thought occurred to him that maybe grown-ups perpetuate a myth of the outside world being a cruel, hard place in which to get by as a means of keeping kids at home. So far, his flight from the nest was smooth sailing. Instead of finding a dark, evil world waiting to prey upon the poor, lost runaway, he found a light, breezy bunch of runaways exploiting the runoff from a lost, confused, wasteful, guilt-ridden society. Willy's natural charm and cute bad-boy style flourished in his new surroundings. He was quick to become a recognized regular. The shopkeepers and the vendors, the cops, and the street people, and the two-bit hustlers—they all took time out to nod a hello at the little guttersnipe. His close association with Black Pat, the well-established well-liked waif and warbler, helped solidify his standing in the community.

Pat was that essential ingredient in a young man's first summer. The sweet and the spice. Willy had never had a girlfriend before, not a real girlfriend. The self-centered focus inherent in the youthful heart allows a pureness of joy that won't come again. And of course, he didn't know that then. The days went by without a thought to whether or not he was doing what he was supposed to. There was no hesitation. He was in love with life, with a heart that was whole. You could see it in his eyes and hear it in his laugh—he was too young to have ever had a broken heart.

Pat was an all together different story. She never let on, but anyone could see it—anyone who had known heartache, that is. It was in her eyes and in her laugh. It was why the neighborhood seemed to look out for her. It was why she always collected twice as much as any of the other street singers on the block. Sure, she had a sweet voice, but there were other sweet voices. There was more to it than that. Even the tourists could see it. They didn't know that her drunken father had made life hell for her and her mother before the bastard finally abandoned them. They didn't know that because of poor health as a child, Pat did most of her growing up in county hospitals. They didn't know that her mother was too sick to scrub floors anymore and that most of the money Pat earned went to help raise her younger brother. Or that a few months before, she almost died after being raped, beaten, and stabbed. Her young eyes held troubles enough for several lifetimes. No matter how bravely she bore up, people saw it.

Except Willy.

That was why she loved him so.

She would pop into Cockroach Art at one in the afternoon and Willy would just be getting up. She'd bring groceries, usually breakfast: juice, coffee, bagels and cream cheese, or dry cereal and milk with a Danish. While he ate she'd get busy cleaning up the place. If both Pats were there, they'd work like a well-coordinated team and have the place tidied up in no time. This seemed only natural to Willy. He grew up with mom to take care of him. That was the way it was, and life goes on.

Only now, he got to make love to Pat. This was something new and wonderful, having it so available. He'd been with girls before; he wasn't a virgin. But he might as well have been. In the old neighborhood, life revolved around the guys.

The first time he got laid, he was thirteen. He knew all about sex, but still hadn't gotten any. He was beginning to worry, to develop a terrible new fear: *What if he got hit by a bus and died before he got to find out what this sex business was all about?* He went with a couple of the guys to a whore. It cost twelve bucks and he'd saved up his ice cream money. It was a milestone outing. He'd been planning it for weeks. His friend's father drove. He asked Willy if his dad knew he was going to a prostitute. Willy told him his father was dead. It did seem an appropriate duty for a father—to take his son. He dropped the guys off and picked them a short time later. He might as well have taken them bowling.

All Willy's encounters with women had been somewhat limited. There was the all too infrequent party where someone's parents went away and left them alone with the house. And once he'd managed to get Angela Gerloven up on the landing of the roof. But there really weren't many opportunities for a project kid to find privacy. There was always the danger that someone would come along and catch them doing what they weren't supposed to be doing. And back then, Willy always had this feeling that he was doing it for the approval of the guys. That macho thing that made it so important to have something to talk about.

This thing with Pat was something else altogether. When he had sex with her, there was nothing else on his mind. They went at each other without knowing how to hold back. She smelled of the coconut oil she put in her hair, mixed with her own dark perfume. He stirred it up real good. He inhaled deeply and was transported out of this world. Which was just as well, since the Cockroach didn't have the most romantic ambiance. There were two bare Sheetrock half-walls separating the sleeping quarters in back from the living room. There were no doors, and sound reverberated throughout the loft.

Early one evening, upon getting back from the Staten Island Ferry—Pat made her best money playing for the commuters—she couldn't wait to be alone with Willy. Chance and Patty were sitting on the couch watching tv. Pat said hello as she practically pulled Willy into the back where the old mattress lay on the floor.

Now Chance had been trying to get into White Pat's pants

for some time. He must have figured that the background sounds of moans and sweaty tones of skin slapping skin might generate the right mood for a successful seduction. He slid over closer to Patty and put his arm around her shoulders and started to kiss her neck. Maybe he was right; she didn't stop him, at least not right away. He was getting a little. He fumbled under her clothes, too busy to notice that she wasn't paying much attention. She was mesmerized by the frenzied pitch coming from behind the thin wall: long bouts of panting punctuated by volleys of cries, a melting sound with a frequency that triggered a longing, an intensity that vibrated goose bumps onto the skin. It went on like that for what seemed an inordinately long time.

Meanwhile, poor Chance! He was a sweetheart, but Patty wasn't quite sure how she ever let it get this far. She never intended... Anyway, she was no cock teaser. He pleaded his way to a hand job, there on the couch. It didn't take long. Willy and Pat were still carrying-on like cats in heat, pounding away and filling the air with unintelligible cries, while Patty was wiping her hand on a Kleenex, grateful that Chance had finished so quickly. She made no effort to hide that she was doing it out of a sense of pity. Chance didn't seem to mind.

To call Chance an easy-going, good-natured neurotic would be an understatement on all counts. But then, to know him was to underestimate him. He inspired perplexity.

For Willy, he proved an invaluable resource, directing him into the quirky, whimsical world of ventriloquism. And even more importantly, Chance was the first person to really value Willy for the skill that he possessed—the skill with voices. In the old neighborhood, he'd never thought of himself as anything special. His talent on two wheels was respected by the younger kids in the projects, but that was kid stuff. This knack with voices, this was something more. Chance was convincing him of that. He provided more than just encouragement, he provided know-how. At the bottom of his prop trunk, Chance had some old books, several L.P.'s and cassettes: *Lessons in Ventriloquism* by Edgar Bergen; Bob Neller; Paul Winchel. And one book entitled *Mouthsounds: Imitations and Special Effects.*

Willy got involved in the material. Really involved. The environment undoubtedly contributed to his zeal. It seemed that everyone in the Village had to have some kind of artistic aspiration in order to justify his life, and his life-style. And an impressionist/ventriloquist—that was a humdinger. In a place where everyone strived for nonconformity, it was unique. It was substantial. It took real dedication to develop, and you had to have ability to begin with. And Willy had it. No doubt about it. Just as there are, on rare occasion, individuals born into our midst who sit down at a piano and, without ever having taken a lesson, begin to play Chopin, Willy Freeman could duplicate voices. He could throw voices. He couldn't combine the two— impersonation and ventriloquism—but then, no one did that— yet.

He worked daily on the exercises in the books to strengthen the muscles of the lips and jaw. These included running through a series of prescribed sounds: *he—ah—oh—who—err—zzzz— zod—mmmmm—ooooo—eeeee—aaaaa—iiiii—yyyyy—nnnnn—ggggg— nnnnnggggg—laaaabambambam*. He would make *click* sounds with his tongue against the hard palate, take a deep breath and expel the air quickly to vibrate the tongue. He would move his tongue in circles in front of his teeth—clockwise and counterclockwise, make a trough with his tongue and stick it out, bite the tip of his tongue, try to swallow his tongue, stretch his upper lip over the lower and vice versa, twist his facial muscles, pout and hold, and relax. Opening his mouth wide, he'd push his tongue against the back of his teeth, pushing harder each time, before letting the jaw and tongue relax. He'd sit in front of a mirror, lips slightly apart in a natural position, teeth a quarter inch apart, or smiling with teeth showing, and try to say certain words without moving his lips—*lady, she, city, train, town, talk, guess, next, test, sack, share, he, they, store, and, they, store, and, thing, there, yes sir!* Practicing the alphabet with his thumb and forefinger between his teeth about a quarter inch into the mouth enabled the tip of the tongue to move freely with the jaw rigid. The sounds were muffled at first, but once the fingers were removed, the sounds were very clear. He practiced changing back and forth from his own voice to the ventriloquial voice. As in singing, proper breathing was stressed and he practiced techniques to correct shallow "chest" breathing. He learned to use substitute letters for the "explosives" or popping lip sounds of *b, p, f,* and *v.* There were other substitutes for the humming sounds of *m.* Illusions aided by misdirection in the muffled voice, the distant voice—these tricks were quickly added to Willy's repertoire as well. Things which normally take months and even years to master—he was progressing at a frightening pace.

One afternoon, Chance had gone out somewhere, and Willy was at Cockroach Art by himself, doing his tongue exercises when White Pat came in.

"Where's Chance?" she wanted to know.

"Not sure. Stick around. ' Probably be back soon."

"That's not why I was asking."

"It's not?"

"No, it's not."

From the way she said it, she didn't have to say any more— but she did. She paused, tilting her head to one side, eyes looking off to the other. She wet her lips and her hand rubbed at the inside of her thigh. "You know... the other night, when you and Pat were in there, and Chance and I was out here?" Willy nodded, he knew. "I want you to do to me what you were doing to Pat."

There was no beating around the bush. Not much thought or discretion either. They tumbled down onto the very same mattress and Willy did his best to recreate the passion and positions that prompted the request for an encore. He wouldn't want to disappoint. After all, this was proof positive—a satisfied customer is the best advertisement. Anything less than the greatest fuck ever would not roost well with his budding ego. ...A regular junior gigolo.

Patty was about the same size as Pat. She had bigger, looser boobs. Oddly enough, once her clothes came off, she seemed a little self-conscious about them. Black Pat never seemed the least bit self-conscious about anything—a natural woman. Patty, despite all her sexual bravado, seemed a touch nervous. Unsure. But that soon fell away and she shook her soft tits and cooed like a bird sitting pretty astride her perch. His hard perch. Bending forward, she showered a slew of kisses onto his face, then sat up and brushed her hair back away from her eyes. Her pupils were enormous; she was beginning to get a faraway look. She didn't gyrate her hips on the same tight "rinse-n-tumble" setting that Black Pat had used. Patty sat all the way down on him, grinding their pubes into a red hot friction. And just when he thought she was about to rub his skin raw, she started to scream, "Oh God! Oh God!" and he felt a soothing wetness pouring out of her. It made a lip smacking, juicy sound each time she moved. It was hot dripping down.

...But it left the sheets cold soaking wet.

Now it was his turn. He lifted her up and turned her over, putting her little butt down on the wet spot. If she minded, she wasn't saying. He put the soles of her feet against his chest and started to pump. A second eruption was set off as he picked up the pace, hard and fast with a low growl rising in his throat. Patty started to scream again, and again a spray of hot, lady-lube flowed fresh between her legs. Willy, too, let go as her contractions tugged on him.

They were both making so much noise, they hadn't realized that there was someone else in the loft. It wasn't until they collapsed, hearts pounding in the stillness of a sweaty embrace, that they heard the *clang* of dishes and the closing of the refrigerator door. They both froze, breath held.

"Who's there?" Willy called out.

There was hesitation—no answer, no movement—then Chance spoke up. He must have felt awkward at having surprised them. It wasn't like he intended to eavesdrop—after all, he did live there.

Willy and Patty dressed quickly. When they came out, they acted like nothing was going on. When they spoke, no one made any eye contact.

Patty said she had to go return a pair of earrings she'd bought, or some such crap. An obvious excuse. Not that it mattered. It would do. She made her exit hurriedly, without a good-bye kiss.

Once she was gone Willy waited for Chance to confront him, chew him out, give him a piece of his mind.

Instead, his mouth full, Chance said, "Willy, you want half a turkey sandwich?"

"What...? Is that all you're going to say? Do I want half a turkey sandwich?"

"I only got the one sandwich. ' Give you half if you want it. What more do you want?"

"You ain't pissed off that I was doing 'the daddy' with Patty? I thought you wanted to be with her?"

"Hey, I don't care. I'm back with Lucrecia. And I have you to thank for it. She doesn't want to have anything to do with that asshole Mark anymore. Your phone call did it."

Chance was grinning like an idiot, pieces of turkey falling out of his mouth. He tore the hero in half and gave the bigger half to Willy.

Willy took it. "You got anything to drink?"

"For the man who helped me win back my true love? Have I got anything to drink?" Chance reached down beside the sofa and brought up a six pack of beer. "Have I got anything to drink!"

~~~

Chapter 12

When you're hot, you're hot.

—American Proverb

Willy was finding it hard to pull himself away from the mirror. His hands patted his hair in homage. Pat had done an incredible job. Black Pat, that is. The thick dark tangle of untamed locks were partitioned and spiked. Glistening strands of hair stood in carefully planned disarray. Twin silver streaks raced back from the temples. Looking good! One bad mother...! His mother would never let him out of the house like this: punker hairdo, dangling fang earring, leather vest—no shirt underneath, jeans strategically shredded and tucked into high leather boots. But she didn't matter anymore. He was a man now. At fifteen. He was stepping out with his ladies. Big night. This was the night he was going to try out his act at Star City.

The boots were borrowed from Chance. The earring came from Gypsy. The vest was a gift from both Pats.

Willy had no idea how, where, or when it happened, but Pat and Patty had apparently discovered they had more in common than just their names. For the time being at least, they seemed to have come to some kind of uneasy understanding: they would share. So the vest seemed to signify. They must have gotten it from one of the leather craftsman on 8th Street. It was absolutely beautiful. All handmade.

"It's time to go line up. Let's get a move on," Jason squeaked up at everybody.

It was real unusual to hear the little fella so wide-awake. He almost never talked. When he did, it was usually a whisper to mommy. Seemed to Willy that even Jason was excited about his first appearance. Willy thought about the pictures out in front of Star City. He thought about his picture taking its place next to the others along that wall of famous faces. He gave one last look in the mirror. Freeze-frame. He would be the best looking star on that wall.

Banded together, their small procession walked at a nice clip down Bleecker, turned up MacDougal, and arrived at Star City just as they were letting everybody in. Perfect timing. Now all he needed was the luck of the draw, a good slot for his first shot.

"I'm nervous already," he said to no one in particular.

"Don't be a silly Willy," said little Jason. "You're gonna be great."

This kid was something else. For weeks, not a peep out of him, and now suddenly he's not only talking to Willy, he's reassuring him. Jason motioned; Willy bent down. He whispered in his ear. Jason wanted to know if Willy was going to do Huckleberry Hound. Willy winked, thumbs-up. The kid was a fan. It must have happened a few afternoons back, when Gypsy left him at the Cockroach. Willy had been watching cartoons and imitating the voices. He thought the kid was sleeping—guess not.

Willy drew number twenty. Alright!

Now it was over to the Kettle for burgers and beer.

Anywhere else, this crew would have stood out as outlandish. On any other streets, Willy, with his punker hair and getup, would've gotten strange looks and double takes. But this was Greenwich Village. If you went around doing double takes here, you'd wind up with chronic whiplash.

Besides, Willy was hot. The stares he was getting weren't of the believe-it-or-not variety. They were far more enticing and only a dab more discreet. Half the women in the room were giving him the eye. It's like the song says, *Them that's got shall get*. Go figure. When you're alone and available, women piss all over you. If you're with another woman, now they're interested. You must be alright; after all, she's with you. They need that corroboration. Even if they don't know the other woman from Eve, it's the *Good Housekeeping* Seal of Approval. And Willy had two. At one point they were both sitting in his lap—Pat, Pat.

The girls in the Kettle weren't the only ones looking: Two guys sitting at the bar weren't missing any of it because, truth was, lately, they were both missing it—they wished they were getting it. They looked to be in their thirties. Despite summer, the thinner of the two wore a flannel shirt. His shoulder length hair was ponytailed. His buddy next to him fit the redneck stereotype: crew cut, stocky, beer-bellied.

Under his breath, so that only Ponytail could hear: "Lucky

son of a bitch got two girls fussin' over him. What's he got? Just a kid. And that hair, like a porcupine pansy."

"Girls go for that shit. Cute pretty boy types. But I tell you something. When you see two girls hanging all over one guy like that, it means he ain't gettin' either one of 'em.

"Yeah, maybe you're right."

"You bet I'm right. Wouldn't be surprised if he's a fairy."

To add to all the eyes aimed in Willy's direction, the absolutely beautiful Lucrecia was sitting directly across the table from him. She was sitting right next to Chance. Not that that mattered. Willy tried to avert his eyes, but every time he looked up she was looking right at him.

Fast allies are formed in the face of a common threat. The two Pats quickly rallied. Their uneasy truce in the territorial dispute over Willy formed a united front. As they sat on Willy's lap, their shows of affection and possession were concerted. Though Willy felt himself the beneficiary, each caress and each whisper in his ear was being done for the benefit of the lovely Lucrecia. The message should have been getting through loud and clear, but the flirtatious Latina remained unfazed. In the face of the most scorching glares imaginable, she went right on working her come-on. It was a good thing there wasn't any gunpowder in the room.

Poor Chance, oblivious to the sparks flying all about him, he was just happy to have his wonderful Lucrecia back at his side. Willy found himself staring at him. He certainly wouldn't want to do anything to hurt him. He was so trusting. Or was it just an act? Chance's way of coping?

As for the battle of the eyeballs, even thought it was two against one, actually four against two, the Pats weren't doing so well. Glare as they might, Lucrecia's bedroom eyes didn't let up. That come-hither look was doing its stuff. Even with two girls in his arms, Willy was beginning to get distracted. That's when Lucrecia brought out the big guns. Saying how it was getting so hot in there, she peeled off the loose fitting denim work shirt that she was wearing. Willy's pupils dilated. Underneath she wore only a thin tank top. God, the girl was perfect!

Black Pat didn't waste any time making a hasty retreat. If that's the way she's going to play, so be it, down and dirty. She whispered something to Patty. They giggled. Then they both whispered to Willy. Under the table, in a none-too-subtle move, Pat reached back and grabbed him between the legs. She smiled sweetly. He looked quickly around the room. The jukebox blared. Everyone was busy eating and drinking and talking like no one had noticed the startled look on his face.

One person had.

The three of them got up to go.

Pat turned back and said, "Meet you guys back at Star City," and then sashayed, arm in arm with Willy, out the door; Patty, giggling and wiggling along on his other arm.

Lucrecia would pout for some time.

Willy was definitely right. This was turning out to be a big night. A big night.

Three hours later, it was a packed house when "Willy and His Hand Jive" arrived at Star City. That's what Jay the doorman called him.

"What's this I hear, you're going on tonight?"

"That's what they say, Jay."

Willy extricated himself from the ladies, who were both looking exceptionally lovely, in order to perform a ceremonious series of high-fives and handshakes. Having concluded the salutation, Jay ducked his head down next to Willy's. "Some guy was around asking for you. Said he was a friend of yours."

Willy didn't say anything; he was waiting for Jay to finish. But Jay was momentarily remanded to the job at hand, collecting the cover from some tourists. Once that was done, he turned back to Willy.

"And...?" Willy asked.

"And what?" Jay wasn't long on brains. To him, focus was something cameras did, and concentration was a tv game show.

"This guy, what else did he say? What'd he look like?"

Jay took a moment to register. "Oh, him. He wanted to know when you'd be back. I told him you had to be back soon since you were going on in about an hour. The guy looked like... like he belonged to *Sha-Na-Na*. Carried one of them big obnoxious boom boxes. Had a tattoo of a wolf."

The door to the club swung open as some customers were leaving, and a funky electric guitar riff wound out into the narrow street, reverberating off the buildings.

Willy looked around quickly. He shouldn't have. He already knew what he would see.

There he was, halfway down the block and closing fast. No mistaking him. The box. The walk. The *click* of the taps. And finally, the voice, "Spokes, my man, I thought that was you."

"Wolfee..." was all Willy could say.

"So, Spokes, ain't you gonna introduce me to your friends?"

Pat's instincts were keen. She was already on the defensive. "What this guy call you?"

Willy explained, "Ain't nothing. A nickname. I used to be called Spokes. Long time ago. Don't mean nothing."

"That's right," Wolfee offered. "Spokes and I go way back. Ain't that right, Bro?'

"It ain't *Spokes* anymore," Willy answered.

Jay broke in, "Yeah, he used to be Spokes, now he's Speaks." Jay laughed. Only Jay laughed. "Don't you get it? He used to be Spokes, but now he's Speaks."

They all gave him a look that said, *Jay, shut up.*

Jay's big head drooped from its six foot four inch height like a kid scolded for speaking out of turn. So much for trying to interject a little comic relief.

"So, what do you want Wolfee?" Willy decided to get right to it.

"Is that any way to talk to your old friend? Why do I have to want anything?" Wolfee was trying to act nonplused, and hurt. He was a terrible actor. "I don't want anything."

And with that, Wolfee feigned leaving in a huff and a puff.

It worked. It blew down Willy's defenses. After all, Wolfee was one of the big bad guys that Willy used to look up to, one of the older guys, one of the tough guys. It wasn't long ago that he'd've given anything to be one of the guys. Wolfee had gone only a few steps when Willy pulled him up by the shirttail.

"Hey, Wolfee, I'm sorry. I didn't mean nothing by it. When I heard some guy was around looking for me, I got a little paranoid. That's all."

Wolfee stopped dead in his tracks. "Well..." He looked sideways, sucking on his eyetooth, then he shrugged it off, "Okay, I guess you got reason." He went for his cigarettes. The pack was in its usual place, rolled in his sleeve. He tipped out one for Willy, too. Like it was automatic. "Rosey's still looking for you. If he knew you was here, he'd be down here in a minute. I wouldn't want to be in your shoes, no way."

"But Rosey don't know?" Willy suddenly looked real vulnerable. "You wouldn't tell him, would ya, Wolf?"

"Now why would I do that?"

He actually seemed sincere.

Willy let out an audible sigh of relief.

"Listen, Spok*er*, I gotta go. Just remembered, there's something I gotta do. Here's a *doobie* for later."

He handed Willy a joint. Willy, looking a little surprised, took it and said, "Hey, thanks."

And with that, Wolfee took off.

He left Willy wondering: *What was that all about? How did he find me? Does anyone else know I'm here?*

He wasn't going to worry about that now. He was going on stage in less than an hour. In the meanwhile, he had this joint. It had been a while since there'd been any weed around—it always got a little dry this time of year.

Once inside the Star, Willy found Chance and, sitting down next to him, showed him what Wolfee had placed in his hands. ...In their hands.

They would wait a while, then go outside and smoke it. They'd go around the corner where there was a little winding street, practically an alley, that not many people used. It was very narrow and didn't go far. It started at 3rd Street and wrapped around the block, depositing you right back at Avenue of the Americas. Supposedly, they had filmed parts of the movie *Serpico* on that block. It was a neat block. It had character. There was nothing on the street except for a few funky apartments.

At the end of the block, about fifty feet in from the avenue, a pricey little restaurant maintained a low profile. Wolfee was, at that moment, entering this establishment. It's hard to imagine the likes of Wolfee having any business in a place like that, but—he did indeed have business there.

The maître d' held the menu like a shield to deflect the oncoming aberration. It looked like tattooed biceps with a man attached—definitely not "proper attire."

Wolfee stood and looked the place over, trying to decide whether it met with his approval. It wasn't Wolfee's style. This entire business wasn't his style. But then, being in debt wasn't his style.

Clearing his throat several times, the maître'd said, "Yes, can I help you?" When what he meant was, *Can I help you out of the restaurant?* He was going to have to learn to be more obvious if he had any hope of dissuading Wolfee.

Wolfee pushed right passed him like he wasn't there.

The dining room was arranged for privacy, with frosted amber arches separating the tables and holding the soft light like brandy on the rocks. Wolfee went from table to table with total disregard for the ambiance. The maître'd tagged after him with his uppity nose out of joint. On his fourth try he got the table he wanted. The man seated in the shadows addressed the maître d', "Thank you, Emilio, for showing my guest to the table. Now if you'll be so good as to bring him a drink."

"Make it a double Jack," Wolfee was quick to add.

Out of deference for the man at the table, Emilio was willing to overlook formalities such as a dress code; however, it was unwarranted that he be spoken to in such a manner. He mustered his most aloof expression and to Wolfee he said, "My name is Emilio, not Jack."

"Emilio, I believe my friend here is referring to Jack Daniels. He'd like a double of Jack Daniels."

"Oh... sorry, sir. "I'll have your waiter bring it right away." Feeling rather awkward, Emilio made a hasty departure.

Wolfee tried to get comfortable in his chair. "Don't know how you knew, but you were right. He's here in the Village. I just saw him around the corner at Star City."

"And you telephoned our 'friend'?"

"Like you said."

"And he took the bait?"

"He don't suspect shit, if that's what you mean. He's gonna come down here. That is what you wanted...? For both our sakes, I hope you know what you're doing."

~~~

Chapter 13

Tune in, turn on, drop out.

—Timothy Leary

As soon as Willy turned the corner he felt the swirl of the city fall away; the still of the back street replaced the press of pedestrians. And with it came a heightened awareness. Like a radio with its volume set to compete with highway noise, suddenly transported beyond the din, his senses blared.

He struck a match. It flared and he immediately lifted it to the joint, catching the burn of sulfur in his nostrils. The result—a cross between a cough and a sneeze—blew out the light. Though he hadn't gotten it to stay lit, a slight whiff of the sweet weed hung in the air. Chance was ready with another match. Willy puffed into cupped hands, making sure the joint was well lit—and getting a potent toke before passing it.

"Good shit!" Willy spoke in a throaty manner, holding the smoke in his lungs.

They were walking next to a waist-high wall—concrete with a little wrought iron imbedded on top to keep people from sitting on it—that separated the sidewalk from a stairwell that descended to a basement door. Suddenly, Willy bent forward, holding onto the wall for support.

"You alright?" Chance asked, at the same time passing the joint back to Willy.

Willy nodded, took the joint and took another hit.

As he moved the joint away from his lips, it fell out of his hand. He no longer felt his hand. Everything, including his legs, began to fold in on itself: at first, like an accordion, and then it was like someone had been fooling with the vertical control on a tv. The whole world was on the fritz. He opened his mouth to speak, but nothing came out.

Chance stood trying to figure out what was wrong; then it hit him. This stuff didn't creep up on you like any weed he'd ever smoked. It came on instantly and just took over. His head felt like a four-wall handball court, and somebody was playing with his brain.

They fell forward, clinging to each other like frightened children on a too scary roller coaster. Willy was white knuckles and brown shorts all the way. He didn't actually... but he felt like he was going to... Or maybe he had... and he didn't know it yet. The carpet had been pulled out from under. The world was slipping away. He had to hold onto Chance or he'd be lost.

To someone who didn't know what was going on, the scene might have looked like a couple of randy queers. And as it turned out, who should happen upon the pretty picture but the two guys from the Kettle: Ponytail and Beer Belly.

"See, what'd I tell ya," Ponytail said, sounding satisfied that his notion was confirmed. "I told you he was a fuckin' fruit."

"I guess you were right. So he wasn't fuckin' them girls after all."

"No way. I told ya. It was just a fuckin' show. The girls knew they were safe with him all along. The little bastard's a cocksucker. Probably gonna give this guy head right here on the street, you'll see."

"Not on this street, he ain't. I'm gonna send that cocksucker back to Christopher Street where he belongs." The thickset homophobe clenched his fist and holding it in front of his face said, "You ready for a little fag bashing?"

"I'm right behind you. Let's do it."

As if things weren't confused enough for Willy, he suddenly found himself faced with an angry redneck.

Beer Belly began to knock him around. He threw Willy down on the ground.

It seemed to Willy that he must have been hit very hard, but it didn't hurt at all. Still, he just lay there on the sidewalk. He wasn't going to get up just yet. Things were spinning too fast. Nothing seemed solid. He was only vaguely aware that he was being kicked in the side.

Then, something that the two attackers hadn't figured on: "I wouldn't mess with that boy if I were you." It was Wolfee. He had his hands behind his back and he was leaning forward as he walked, heading straight for them like a torpedo. "The kid's tight with some badass motherfuckers. You would not want to tangle with the people he knows."

The two men turned and stared at the *greaser* who was talking at them.

His inflection brimming with disgust, Beer Belly said, "And who the fuck might that be?"

Wolfee was right up on them now. He got up in Beer Belly's face and said... "Me."

Now it was clear that these two characters were violent. They were making every effort to prove that point to Willy. But when it came to *violent*, they were simply no match for the likes of Wolfee. Here was a real hitter. They were strictly minor league. It only took a second.

Beer Belly went to push Wolfee out of his face. Wolfee moved back a step. With his shoulder, he pushed Ponytail over the wall. It was an eight foot drop. Then, bringing his hand up lightning fast he landed a roundhouse flush on the side of Beer Belly's head. One punch, lights out. He dropped like someone pulled the plug, crumpling straight down.

He was lying next to Willy, and Willy could see where the blow hit. There was blood coming from around his ear.

Wolfee took a step toward the curb and flipped a large chunk of broken cobblestone between two parked cars. He didn't want anyone to see, but Willy saw. No wonder Beer Belly went down like he'd been hit by a brick—he'd been hit by a brick.

Chance stood slack-jawed. Willy felt paralyzed. But as Beer Belly moaned with the gradual return of consciousness, Willy sprung to his feet. The legs which he could not feel boosted him up like a Palooka Joe punching bag.

"Easy does it, Bro," Wolfee cautioned. "Just take it easy, Spokes, my man. You be flustered 'cause you be dusted. But you have the strength of ten."

"What are you talking about?" Willy's words were a garble. They didn't sound that way to him, but the boy of many voices was incoherent.

Wolfee was high on the violence he'd done and he just kept talking. It soon became clear, even to Willy, that the joint was laced with the one drug he'd never wanted anything to do with: angel dust, PCP.

His mind jammed, overwrought with a dozen horror stories he recalled about the unpredictable, often grisly consequences of angel dust: people putting their eyes out, flying out of windows, walking in front of trains, kids killing their parents, mothers killing their babies.

He pushed Wolfee down—that's right!—Spokes pushed Wolfee.

He didn't believe it either. It was all over now. He was done for. He ran like a madman. He didn't think about where he was running, but he retraced his steps and ended up in front of Star City.

As he stood there under the landmark Star City sign, a big vertical stack of lighted letters with a neon star atop, he felt his chest heave trying to catch his breath. Sensation was returning; he was beginning to feel his body. Maybe this meant he was going to be alright. He hadn't committed suicide, murder, or mutilation, and the effect of the dust was lifting. For the first time he noticed his bloody lip and scraped arm. His new leather vest was practically ruined. He couldn't deal with that now. He just wanted to be with Pat.

Jay wasn't at the door; Willy walked right in. Inside the club was dark. Willy's eyes took a moment to adjust.

Laughter spilled from the back room. A standup comic was delivering a hackneyed routine about growing up in a tough neighborhood. The audience played along; in unison, "How tough was it?"

Just then, at the near end of the bar, one of the customers swiveled on his stool. Willy could feel his heart kick into double time. Rosey was at Star City.

A group of folks entering the club was startled by the panic-stricken little freak who pushed past them.

"Hey, Spokes, come back here. I ain't gonna hurt—"

It was no use. He was gone.

Rosey got up, sullen and resolute; the chase was on.

Rosey made no attempt to overtake him, but he kept up enough so as not to lose him.

Thinking he was getting lost in the crowds, praying he was getting lost in the crowds, Willy wasn't looking back.

But the busy sidewalk left an easy to follow trail of turned heads and unwitting tattletales.

"You see a kid with two-tone hair, wearing a vest, run past here?"

The question brought a chorus of *that-a-way* and a volley of pointing fingers.

Willy should've tried harder to shake him; after all, he knew he was being followed. But Rosey, on the other hand, had no reason to suspect *he* was being followed. No one ever thinks that the one doing the following is himself being followed. Two shadows tread close behind—one moved on pointy Puerto Rican cockroach killers and the other on patent leather—around a few corners, down a few streets, through a small parking lot filled with bakery trucks, through a hole in a fence, to the back door of the abandoned factory that housed Cockroach Art.

From a distance, Rosey spied his quarry duck into the condemned building.

Once inside, Willy leaned his back against the door, closed his eyes, and sobbed. He was alone and he was hidden and he needed a good cry. He'd been working so hard at being a man. Now he felt like a lost boy. The tears rolled. They streaked his dirty face, and he rubbed his eyes and wiped his cheeks with dirty hands. His head hurt and his nose was stuffed, but some of the fear was lifting. He slid down the door to sit on the floor, spent and momentarily released from the turmoil.

Very momentarily. The door jerked open, sending him toppling back. Instantly the dread was back. A stifled scream reverberated inside his brain.

But wait—a reprieve. The padlocked chain prevented the door from opening fully. Willy thought, *Thank you, God. Thank you for that chain.* His gratitude may have been a little premature as a hand reached in and grabbed him.

"Gotchya."

Rosey latched onto the vest. Willy tried to pull away, flailed about, but it was no use. He had too strong a grip.

Then Willy slipped out of the vest. Simple as that.

As he raced to the elevator, he could hear Rosey tugging on the door. It wouldn't keep him out for long, just slow him down. He'd manage to squeeze through.

Damn elevator was taking forever. He thought he heard footsteps. He did hear footsteps. He decided to take the stairs.

The stairwell was dark and littered with trash; the air, stale and stuffy. The stairs were metal and resounded, each step like the *pinging* of a sonar blip in a submarine hunt. How had he managed to get himself into such deep water!

He heard the door to the stairwell open, saw the faint red glow of the hall lights. One landing up, he didn't move a muscle, sweat practically peeing from his pores.

Rosey *clicked* his cigarette lighter, shedding a little light on the situation. His eyebrows twitched up and he squirted spit between his teeth.

Willy was concentrating so hard his lips were mouthing his thoughts, *Please God, make him go 'way. Please, oh please.*

Rosey started up the stairs.

Willy broke and took off running. He held onto the banister as he rounded the flights. Now Rosey was running too. And he was gaining. As Willy opened the door onto the fifth floor, Rosey reached the landing. He passed through the door right behind Willy and reaching out, he spun him around.

He was cornered. He lashed out.

But Rosey didn't fight back; he merely shielded himself. He tried several times to catch Willy's hands, but then Willy would start kicking. Then one punch actually landed. A wild overhand, right on the button, caused Rosey to step back holding his nose. They were both stunned by the blow—Rosey by the impact; Willy, that he had done what he did.

Rosey let him have it. It was a backhand slap, but it lifted Willy off the ground and sent him sailing through the air.

A blurry vision of Rosey bending over him was the last thing Willy remembered.

The next thing he knew there were a lot of people bending over him. His head was slow to clear, at first letting in the unreal red light of Cockroach Art, then the reassuring sounds of familiar voices, friends' voices.

Somebody said, "Make room. Give him some air."

"What happened?" Willy asked.

They all moved in closer, speaking among themselves: "He said something." "What'd he say?"

Pat asked him, "You okay, baby?"

"Yeah, I think so. What happened?"

"You don't remember nothing that happened?"

"I remember fighting with Rosey. I hit him right in the nose. That's all I remember."

Willy was beginning to see clearer now, and he could see the worry on his friends' faces. Of course they were concerned if he was alright. But there was something else going on here. For what seemed like a very long time, nobody said anything.

Then Chance spoke up, "So you don't remember throwing him down the elevator shaft...? Holy shit, it's just like all those stories you hear, about people when they're on angel dust.... Gives them the strength of ten men."

~~~

Chapter 14

One's own escape from troubles makes one glad; but bringing friends to trouble is hard grief.

—Sophocles

A few feet from where Willy was lying unconscious was the elevator shaft. Like a passageway to the dark side, it opened onto Willy's new reality. He had been knocked out for only a minute, but nothing would be the same ever again. The freight elevator hung a foot and a half below the landing. Atop the car was one heavy lading to carry; Chance shined a flashlight on the dead man. It was Rosey alright. Or rather, Rosey—not at all alright.

Willy didn't know if he found him scarier alive or dead. He half expected Rosey at any moment was going to raise his eyebrows and squirt spit between his teeth.

Willy wasn't the only one scared shitless. The others had been on their way to find Willy. They had just started up in the elevator when Rosey crashed down on top of it. According to Patty, he didn't die instantly; they had to listen to his death moans echo in the shaft as they made their ever so slow ascent.

Jason was crying; Gypsy tried to comfort him. Patty couldn't stop babbling. Chance was upset that he'd have to share his loft with a dead man. Lucrecia was... Lucrecia. She looked out a loft window to the street below, coldly disinterested.

She was a strange one—not particularly smart—but when you look that good, people overlook a lot. She seemed totally unaffected by it all. Hard to imagine being so blasé after having just had a person fall to his death on top of you.

Only Pat seemed scared for Willy. If she was at all scared for herself, it was that she might lose him. She brought a cold compress to hold to his head, and she held him close as he shivered. She told him that everything was going to be alright; she almost sounded as if she believed it.

It was Pat who took charge of the situation. She made it clear that no one was to say a word about any of this to anyone. She made everyone swear to it. Even Jason. Especially Lucrecia.

They moved the body into the subbasement. Chance took the arms; Willy and Pat took the feet. Chance was the only one who had been down there before. The building had a multilevel substructure with a cold storage dug into the bedrock. Willy thought it was like descending into hell.

When he came up out of there he knew he had to run away. It was the kind of panic that sets in when you're suffocating. His friends agreed, Willy was going to have to leave town for a while. They hurriedly gathered up whatever they could: money, a sleeping bag, an old knapsack, a warm sweater. It wasn't much, but it would all come in handy.

* * * * *

Before he knew it, he was standing in Port Authority waiting for a bus.

The decision to have Pat go with him was a last minute thing. She was telling him how she knew she'd never see him again, how whenever she cared for something it got taken away. She wasn't saying it to feel sorry for herself; it was just the way it was. *Not this time*, thought Willy. She'd been so good to him; he wanted to do something for her. Not to mention that he desperately needed a friend. So he said that she could come along if she wanted and she reacted like he was doing her a favor.

As the Greyhound got out past the early morning rush feeding lines of commuter cars into the city, sheer exhaustion gave way to fitful sleep. Pat covered Willy using her jacket for a blanket.

From then on Willy would find difficulty sleeping. He used to sleep like a log, straight through the morning to twelve, one in the afternoon. He used to have no trouble taking a nap around four-thirty, five. No more. That was B.R.—Before Rosey.

Adolescence is difficult enough just learning to deal with the usual emotions of love and jealousy without having to come to grips with guilt. Big-league, killed-a-man kind of guilt. And not just any man. This was a man that a boy looked up to. This was the man that this fatherless boy had turned into a hero. He would have to wrestle with this burden. Time would pass, the miles would pass—the burden wasn't going to get any lighter. He was just going to have to get stronger.

* * * * *

Halfway across the country and the only thing keeping him from being crushed under the weight of his burden was to just keep going.

As might be expected under the circumstances, he didn't prove the most pleasant of travel companions. Still, Pat was patient and caring. She was one to stand by her man. Even when that meant standing alongside a hot dusty highway at high noon trying to thumb a ride.

They'd taken the bus as far as their money would take them. Left off in the middle of nowhere, they found themselves in a rough spot. The highway sped around hills and bends. If any cars passed this way—and it didn't look like many did—they were going too fast to slow down. And even if they did manage to spot the hitchhikers before they were right on top of them, the way they looked wasn't likely to further their odds. Here was a pair of fish out of water: an eighteen year old black chick in cutoffs and high heels, and a fifteen year old white boy with two-tone spiked hair—in the middle of the boonies. It was beginning to feel like they'd never get a ride out of there when the rainbow van approached—a rainbow, like a gentle waterfall of colors, painted on the side.

The guy in the passenger seat said for them to take off their shoes before getting in. Without getting out, he slid open the side panel door, then ducked back behind a translucent weave of curtain separating the cab from the rest of the van. Willy didn't get a good look at him, but he'd have to be blind not to notice that the guy was a Hare Krishna: orange robe, shaved head. And he'd have to be deaf not to hear that Southern accent, thick as biscuits and gravy.

The back of the van was carpeted, the walls hung with bells and beads. The smell of burning incense permeated the place.

Willy and Pat took off their shoes and got in. Beggars can't be choosers.

They rolled back onto the highway with a *jangle* like the sound of a thousand miniature church bells, or temple chimes, or the *clang* of a small junk wagon. Take your pick, whatever your persuasion.

Nobody said anything; they just rode along in silence—if you can call being locked inside a rolling wind chime *silence*. It was like you weren't supposed to say anything. Willy didn't know why it felt that way, it just did.

When Willy finally heard the two men talking softly to each other, he decided to try to join the conversation—the usual talk: "Hi, I'm Willy, and this is Pat. Thanks for giving us a ride."

No response.

"Nice van!"

Still nothing.

"How far you guys going?"

It was a direct question; they had to say something.

It was the driver who answered: "This is Harry and I'm..."

139

there was a hesitation as though he had to decide what to call himself, "...Steve. We're going to Las Vegas."

"Harry and Steve?" Willy repeated.

Harry apparently took objection: "Harry and Steve. Anything wrong with that?"

Willy felt himself push against the wall of the van. "No, nothing. I was just checking to make sure I heard correctly, is all.... It's kinda noisy in here... with the bells and all...."

"You heard correctly." He said it like an indictment. "And you know what my last name is...?"

"No, Harry... What's your last name?" Willy wasn't at all sure he wanted to know.

"Krishna. Harry Krishna." He laughed like a looney-tune. Then, as if to squelch any further attempt at conversation, Harry started hitting a small drum that he was holding in his lap and chanting:

Harry Krishna

Harry Krishna

Harry Harry

Harry Krishna

Harry Rama

Harry Rama

Krishna Krishna

Rama Lama Ding Dong...

It wasn't any chant Willy ever heard. And the guy had a crummy voice and a lousy sense of timing to boot. To make matters worse, the driver joined in, and he was chanting something a little different:

Hare Krishna

Hare Krishna

Hare Hare

Hare Hare

Hare Rama

Ama Gonna

Rama Rama

Rama Your Momma

Hare Krishna

Hare Krishna

Krishna Krishna

Little Black Momma…

Willy couldn't believe what he was hearing. Was this the way Hare Krishna's talked when they were by themselves?

He looked across to where Pat was lying. She was fast asleep. Oblivious to everything. She must have been exhausted to sleep through this.

The drumming continued, louder and faster. There was more whispering up front. Then the curtain moved.

Willy quickly faked disinterest, yawning as though he too was fading off to sleep. He lowered his eyes, but not before first stealing a glimpse of his hosts. It was the driver who pushed aside the curtain. A beefy arm, blue with tattoos. The reflection in the rearview mirror revealed that he was not shaved completely bald like his friend, but had short cropped skinhead style hair and clothes. Willy also got a frightening glimpse of

Harry, who turned to check on his passengers, like a captor checks on his prisoners. Those were not the spacey glazed-over eyes of a Hare Krishna. Something was very wrong here.

It suddenly came to Willy: *Somewhere behind them, in a ditch at the side of the road, must be one pale skinny dead guy minus his orange robes and van.*

Once the curtain fell back into position and the two "imposters" had their eyes forward again, Willy tried to wake Pat. She was out like a light. He shook her until he got a groggy response. Covering her mouth, he whispered in her ear, "We're in some deep shit."

She answered with, "Uh, we are? Okay... deep shit," and went right back to sleep.

While Pat was off in dreamland, for Willy, the rest of the ride with the Krishna thugs became a waking nightmare. His mind raced through stories of hitchhikers who were never heard from again. Lately the newspapers were filled with such stories, of sickos who cruised the highways looking for victims for their sadistic torture. His heart pounded in his throat as he made believe he was asleep and waited for the worst. They drove on like that for hours—some of the longest hours Willy ever knew.

Daylight was dwindling when the van pulled into a gas station. Dozens of little black birds flitted from their perch on the gas station sign to the grey sky and back again. The attendant moseyed over.

This was the break Willy needed. Pat had just woke up; she sat up, stretching her arms and looking around. Willy made his move for the door.

"I can use to stretch the ol' legs a bit," he told Harry, who was eyeing him like a hawk. "Come on, Pat, maybe you gotta use the rest room. Might not get another chance for a while."

As they started toward the building, Willy turned back and scooped up Pat's knapsack. "Better take this. You might want your toothbrush or something, change of underwear, or female stuff."

He was jabbering like a nervous fool. But he wasn't fooling anyone. The Krishna thugs both squinted menacingly as their eyes followed the departure of their would-be fun and game.

"Pat, we got to get away from those guys. They're not what you think," Willy explained quickly. "I overheard them talking while you were sleeping."

It didn't take much convincing; once Pat was told what they were chanting, there was no way she was going back into that van.

The rest rooms were located to the back and side of the building. Willy really did have to go but decided he'd have to hold it. *Get while the getting was good.*

They ran behind the station and kept on running behind several other buildings till they came to a rural back road. It ran perpendicular to the main highway. They were both out of breath and changed from a run to a fast walk, looking back every so often. They had no idea where they were, or where this road went—as long as it went away from those two phonies and the rainbow van.

Ahead, to either side, there were several clusters of houses spaced wide apart and set back off the road. They were clearly visible in the dusk, like outcroppings of boulders on the virtually treeless landscape. But they were some distance off, with nothing but desolation in between.

They heard an engine shifting gears up the hill behind them. Maybe they'd get lucky.

They turned to see the rainbow van appear on the horizon. They were after them. In the rapidly gathering dusk the headlights angled down at the road, searching like the snoot of a bloodhound on a fresh scent.

There was no place to hide. They ran along the rutty dirt and gravel shoulder, stumbling down the side of the road as the van swooped down upon them. It jerked to a stop and instantly orange-robed Harry and his friend jumped out and started to chase them.

An old saying that Willy's mother used to use came to mind: *There are no free rides in this world.* It certainly looked like there was going to be a high price to pay this time. Given the circumstances, with fear crackling across the synapses, it was a mighty peculiar function of the brain to say *I told you so* at a time like this.

Willy was tackled from behind. Hare Krishna's are known to be a little pushy, but this was ridiculous; the guy was pushing Willy's face into the ground, digging his knee into Willy's back.

He shouted, "I got him. Steve, you get the girl."

The girl, however, wasn't being very cooperative. Ever since

144

the time she was jumped in Harlem, Pat always carried a knife, a nasty little number. The black stiletto released its five inch blade. Even in the moonless night, there was enough light to reflect the glint of steel. Steve stopped in his tracks.

"My little Tar Baby got herself a shiv," Steve shouted to Harry. "Ain't it just like a nigger..."

Harry repeated, "Tar Baby..." and laughed.

Beads of perspiration appeared on Steve's brow. But the eyes and the grin said it was excitement, not fear.

Pat held the knife at arm's length and slashed at the air. They did a little cha-cha to and fro and sideways, momentarily caught in an invisible restraint that maintained a constant distance between them. Pat knew it wasn't going to hold for long. She rushed him.

One of the prevailing arguments against carrying a weapon is that, if you're not properly trained in the use of that weapon, it is likely to be used against you. Pat had purchased the knife in a 42nd Street emporium. It had given her a sense of security.

Steve easily sidestepped the lunge, put a hold on Pat, and broke her grip. His arm went 'round her neck. She noticed one of the tattoos: a swastika with the words *White Power*. She started kicking and punching, putting up an admirable fight. He picked up the knife and pressed the blade to her throat. She went limp. The blade's power to persuade cuts deep when reinforced by past experience. Having death poised just a slash away took the fight out of her body. Her mind was seething with rage.

Willy watched as Steve, the skinhead, took Pat to the van.

"Steve, save some for me." Harry Krishna laughed like a looney-tune. "Steve, save some for me. Be right there... soon as I take care of her little friend here."

The skinhead told him, "Take your time," before he disappeared into the rainbow van.

There was a sinking feeling inside Willy that left his heart hollow.

~~~

Chapter 15

...by the skin of my teeth.

—*Job 19:20*

Inside the van, the bells, beads, and bobbles shook in a cruel laughter at Patricia Reed.

She was pushed down onto the floor. She searched the face of her attacker. There would be no appealing to any spark of decency in those cold grey eyes. She knew too well that after—when they were through raping her—she would be killed. She didn't want the last thing she saw to be ugly and hateful.

The skinhead ripped her blouse.

She closed her eyes and tried to block out what was happening. They would do what they wanted with her body, but her mind would be elsewhere.

The knife cut open the front of her bra. She felt the blade nick a red line between her breasts. He balled up the flimsy fabric, shoved it into her mouth, and tied it in place.

She felt a strange relief—she wasn't going to have to give him head; he couldn't very well force her to suck his dick if she had a gag in her mouth.

Using the belt from his pants he tied one of her hands to the inside of the sliding door panel. He used a coarse piece of rope to tie the other, attaching her outstretched arm to a strong metal hook under the front seat. He left her feet untied; he still had to get her shorts off.

Pat concentrated hard, her mind coming to rest on a memory—an early memory, of five or six years old.

It had always been perplexing to Pat that she had no recollections of being a child. It was as if her life began at thirteen. She knew that other people remembered back, or at least they said they did. When she tried, there was nothing—no birthday parties, no first day at school, no little friends. No nothing.

From where was this image suddenly drawn? She wondered if it was ever real, or a fantasy she'd dreamed up and carried in her subconscious—the photograph of a model family that comes in a new picture frame when you buy it. Only now did it spread itself out in front of her: a picnic at Coney Island with her mom and her dad. The wicker basket was full of sweet corn, Southern fried chicken, sweet potato pie, and watermelon. The sky was swept clear of clouds by the breezes up high and stood out against the sunlit air, an uninterrupted sheet of blue—apart from several kites flitting upon its surface, and an occasional plane. There were no sounds in her memory. Just pictures, and smells. Ah, the smells. Nothing develops an appetite like ocean air.

The brain never really rests. Even when seemingly lost in the deepest sleep it continues to survey innumerable bits of information, deciding to disregard all but the most urgent of signals. An exhausted mother may sleep right through the most intolerable racket, only to wake instantly at the soft keening of her infant. So it was that a cry penetrated into the barrier of Pat's dream, dispersing her refuge, disallowing her denial.

Her eyes snapped open, welling up with tears that overflowed down her cheeks. Her heart moved closer to her head—getting stuck near her throat.

It was Willy. He was hollering like a dying siren.

Pat forgot she was helpless, tied and gagged; she started fighting again, tugging on her bonds, kicking like a wildcat.

The skinhead was caught off guard. A couple of solid kicks landed; he was knocked back against the rear of the van. Out of range, he stood there with a blank look on his face—like he forgot why he was there. Then he looked down at the knife waiting in his hand.

"Tar Baby... ain't love a bitch."

With both hands he held the blade out and moved toward her.

A rapping on the outside of the van, against the metallic wall, reverberated, emphasizing how closed in they were—little Patricia and this sicko skinhead with the knife.

"Steve, come quick. You got to see this." It was Harry Krishna and he was laughing his looney-tune laugh. "Hurry, Steve!"

He broke off his menacing approach without a word. His thin lips almost smiled as if to say, *I'll be right back.* He turned, slid open the side door, and stepped out.

"Over here, Steve. Hurry."

Harry Krishna's voice carried on the wind. Steve could see the orange robes in the distance. It appeared he was running toward the van, but in the darkness Steve wasn't sure. He jogged a few steps from the roadside and peered into the pitch-black.

He didn't see Willy roll out from under the van into the driver's seat. The keys were right there in the ignition. Before the skinhead could realize what was happening, Willy started her up, and was taking off.

...From where those two Krishna thugs stood, on the barren high plains road, it must've seemed like they could see those taillights forever through the cold crystal night air.

Once again Willy's talent for voices had come into play. Sandals aren't meant for running; and once he'd given 'ol Orange Robe the slip, he ran, cloaked by moonlessness. Good thing for Willy that Harry was not only slow on the flats, but upstairs as well. A scream trailing off into the night served to misdirect. Willy doubled back to the van. He had no problem imitating the Dixie accent Harry Krishna used to call Steve. Or the looney-tune laugh.

And now he and Pat were racing cross-country, their own van, a full tank of gas—and, as it turned out, a pot of gold at the end of the rainbow van.

In the armrest console alongside the driver's seat, Willy found a canvas bag. In the bag was ten thousand dollars.

~~~

Chapter 16

The efforts which we make to escape from our destiny only serve to lead us into it.

—Ralph Waldo Emerson

As far as Willy and Pat could tell, it was a day like any other.

To the forces of nature here on earth, it was phenomena as usual: photosynthesis, the oxygen cycle, the never-ending rapacity of the food chain. And to the gods in the heavens, this particular day did not outwardly appear to herald deviation from their accustomed indifference which the mortal marking of time has come to record.

But to those who had gathered in the high desert, it was to be a truly new day, the beginning of a New Age. They had come to Arizona in observance; they were pioneers on the frontier of consciousness.

The wind played with the sand, kicking up dust devils and scooting them across the mesa. As the sun arced through the heavens it whitewashed the hallowed ground and made the air brittle. As the light of the new day ascended upon the meticulously calculated geographic latitude of the observers, the rainbow van was observed riding over the horizon.

Pat had been driving all night, somewhat lost, and glad to see people. Now she could find out where in the middle of nowhere she was and get directions. While she was at it, she'd find out what in the world all these people were doing out there.

The road ended in a profusion of cars and campers waiting at the bony face on the edge of tomorrow. Amid no houses or accommodations an assemblage had convened, like a tailgate party that had lost its way.

The shimmer lifting off the surface of the road made the rainbow van appear to be riding on air.

"Willy," Pat called, reaching back to nudge her lover boy, "take a look at this!"

He had been resting comfortably, wrapped in a cocoon of bright orange. His own clothes were too rank even for him, and the only thing he could find to wear was Hare Krishna garb. The van came with a roof rack which came with a trunk full of all sorts of stuff from India: clothes, jewelry, books, incense.

Willy came up front and pondered at the landscape of men and women standing in the dry dawn radiance. All facing the same direction, they brought to mind *Close Encounters of the Third Kind*—although it wasn't clear, *Who were the aliens?*

Pat pulled over onto the side of the road.

Before the dust had settled, a welcoming committee from the anomalous congregation approached. They were all smiling. It was a truly diverse delegation: clear-eyed gray-haired emissaries from health food stores, frosted and half-baked old tarts, three-piece motivational gurus, Zen entrepreneurs—purveyors of pyramids and crystals, and children with names like *Moonbeam* and *Galaxy*.

Willy considered rolling up the window. Maybe get the hell out of there fast.

Too late. Pat was out of the van, accepting a flower from a towheaded child and his mom.

Willy sat perfectly still, the way you're supposed to when confronted by a strange dog. He didn't asking himself why he was acting so unsociable. Neither did anyone else.

When the welcome wagon eventually left, Pat got back into the van. She was able to fill Willy in: "These people have all come here to celebrate something they call the *Harmonic Convergence*; it's some kind of major event in the heavens that is going to mark the beginning of a New Age of Enlightenment on earth.

And though this was the first Pat had heard about it, she believed in this sort of thing and wanted to stay. Besides, these folks had been nice enough to invite them to a big vegetarian dinner planned for that evening.

Willy always liked to party; she did say it was a celebration. It wasn't like they had anywhere they had to be. Besides, they'd been non-stop for three states. A rest stop was in order. So after Pat and Willy played a little rock-the-van, it was nap time.

About half-past the sundial, they got the wake-up call from Hotel Horoscope; there was a Tibetan gong situated on the edge of the encampment and its reverberation rolled unobstructed over the guests of the desert to be absorbed in the stillness beyond, waves into sand.

The groups' activities were being coordinated by a positively ancient woman who was called Aunt Dorethea. She didn't directly tell everyone what to do, but rather let her will be known through her inner circle of followers. Throughout the day she conducted private audiences inside her recreational vehicle. Aunt Dorethea this, Aunt Dorethea that—she was in everyone's conversation.

Willy didn't know what to make of it. So much had happened, their trip cross-country was beginning to seem more like a journey through different worlds: from a maze of narrow tenements to a puzzle of stargazers holding hands under an open sky. It's one thing to take the boy out of the city... Nevertheless, Willy went along with the program: he sat cross-legged and meditated; he smiled at everyone and everything; he took his place in the aerial map of enlightened souls arranged on the desert floor as a signpost to the Coming of a Higher Consciousness, of a New Age—wouldn't want it to lose its way. And by the time nightfall switched on the electric ceiling that bedazzles high above the desert, with all of the positive vibrations around him, Willy's deep-seated hard-edged New York skepticism was softening just a bit. Several small campfires contributed a warm glow. Many people brought out lanterns.

Dinner turned out to be a pot-luck affair. Help yourself, smorgasbord style. Pat felt badly that she didn't have anything to contribute. But it was really alright. They were guests. And as such they were treated with geniality and seated at a long table with Aunt Dorethea and about thirty others: an honor.

Seated on Willy's left was Greta Gilmore—*Greta the Gregarious*. She was an old dame, wore a lot of makeup and a wide-brim hat. She was quick to volunteer that she was sixty-eight years old, a widow, and a longtime follower of Aunt Dorethea's. She was only too thrilled to act as Pat and Willy's guide to the gathering.

"That's Bruce Wilson," she whispered, indicating the boyish silver fox at Aunt Dorethea's right hand. "He's Aunt Dorethea's personal secretary. Any minute now he's going to stand up and lead the saying of grace.

It is the tendency to see the world in terms of one's own bailiwick. Thus the tailor notices the cut of your suit; the dentist, your overbite. Willy's ear for sounds was growing sharper every day. Greta had a voice turned green from jealousy. He heard ambition in her rhythm and an uncertainty in her end syllables.

Despite the telltale resentment, Greta was really quite charming. Her new young friends found themselves liking her. She was the quintessential gossip. The newcomers had latched onto the grapevine and the wine... it flowed and flowed: The Atlantis Fellowship, as they were sometimes called, has for centuries been comprised of the same members who tend to reincarnate in cycles; these were all old friends known to each other in previous sojourns dating back to the Lost City of Atlantis, or so the story went.

Willy and Pat digested this extraordinary information

between bites of homemade bread and tofu salad, steamed veggies and brown rice.

But there was more: the highlight of the meal, the main dish, the spiritual sustenance—Aunt Dorethea would channel the guide and spirit teacher known as *Sayer*, a fourth dimensional entity from the star system Arcturus.

While Greta got momentarily sidetracked in a plate of tofu Napolitano and zucchini bread, Willy whispered to Pat, "You think maybe somebody spiked the herb tea with acid?"

"Now be nice," she scolded. She fixed a sidelong glower on him that had him sitting up straight for the remainder of the meal.

After the dishes were cleared away and the brisk chitter-chatter had worn itself down to a dawdling chitchat, it was time.

But first, Bruce announced, "I'd like to welcome two newcomers with us tonight." He motioned for Willy and Pat to please stand.

In her most demure manner Pat offered, "Hi, I'm Patricia Reed."

Everyone applauded enthusiastically, as if she had made a statement with which they all agreed. She reflexly took a little curtsy.

Willy was acting strange. He stood but did not say a word, so Pat volunteered, "...And this is Willy Freeman."

Again, warm applause as they both sat back down.

A microphone and amplifier were set up alongside Aunt Dorethea. She didn't stand before her devotees; she seemed almost too frail. Instead Bruce brought the microphone to her and the moment she took hold of it—quiet. Everyone leaned forward a few inches. Willy noticed a young woman click on a portable tape recorder. Several lanterns were placed by the old lady, their brightness seemed to grow exponentially. *Must be some kind of illusion or special effect—the total being greater than the sum of its parts.*

Willy looked over at Pat. She was completely enthralled, hanging on the promise of enlightenment.

As Aunt Dorethea started speaking, the magic that had been built on anticipation and the carefully choreographed sense of drama teetered. Here was somebody's grandmother. A wrinkled little saccharine voice extolling her gratitude on her many beautiful grandchildren who have dutifully come to visit—*Could this really be the person all the fuss was about?* Willy scanned the crowd trying to gauge the sway. No one else seemed to be the least bit put off by grandma. Worry lines pinched his brows; he thought, *I must be missing something.*

Aunt Dorethea was speaking disjointedly, extolling the virtues of knowing your feelings, reaching your goals, and most importantly, being kind to others and to yourself. All very innocuous advice. Then there was something about how all this would become easier now that the New Age of Light was upon us. You could barely hear her now, despite the microphone. The old broad was falling asleep. In the middle of her discourse. Willy couldn't believe it. She couldn't even stay awake long enough to finish what she was saying. He was about to make some remark,

157

but Greta was quick to hush him. All around everyone was motionless, their eyes still fixed on their antediluvian avatar who sat before them, lost in the Land of Nod.

Her head did not raise up off her chest and though her voice resounded, her lips did not appear to move; it was as if she were talking in her sleep: "There is one here in spirit who would speak with those that are present physically, if they desire to so communicate."

Willy thought it was one slick piece-a'-work. *She was a first-rate ventriloquist. Someone had boosted the PA as she was throwing her voice. Or maybe it was a tape recording*—that's what he thought. But he could barely hear himself think as the Gathering answered Aunt Dorethea in near unison, "We desire at his time to have that which would be given." *Wow!—so much for counterculture.*

Aunt Dorethea's breathing was beginning to change. The expression on her face was also changing: small strained movements of the lips and the muscles of the face suggesting the efforts of the incoming entity to gain control. From Lord only knows where inside that bent and bone-depleted old bag, she found enough skeleton to sit up straight—not just hold herself with added poise, but sit military-posture erect. Her eyelids snapped open revealing a faraway look in her eyes and, in a voice that was neither male nor female, she greeted the Gathering as Sayer:

Hail to beings of the physical plane. I greet you in love and peace. I congratulate you upon reaching this auspicious crossroads on your spiritual journey. The stars of your galaxy

158

presented you with a transcendent vibration and you were ready in place and time to welcome in an era of unparalleled spiritual prosperity. The harmony would not have been complete without your voices. You are the vanguard of higher consciousness. I see wonderful things happening in your reality. The gradual metaphysical awakening of your civilization during the past decades will gain momentum and open your eyes to the light. The light is love, and love is the light. Be enlightened... I will hear now from my brothers and sisters in light who seek guidance.

At this point, certain individuals in the group started to jockey for place; you could see the effort put forth to restrain themselves from calling *Pick me, pick me*, like an audience at a tv game show. Only by drawing upon their reverence and veneration for Aunt Dorethea were they able to sustain the serenity. No one dared break the trance, and risk losing the cosmic connection.

In a barely audible whisper, "Do you feel what I feel?" Pat inquired of Willy.

There was no denying it. The hairs on the back of his neck were standing on end, like when someone walks over your grave: just an old superstition his mother used to tell him. Maybe it was some kind of mass hypnosis. Whatever it was... he looked at Pat and didn't say a word.

Aunt Dorethea, or rather Sayer, began to hum. It was an amorphous little ditty like a creaky door opening.

Then, the first name was called: "Cheryl Hunt."

A bland young wallflower suddenly came to life. She stood up and came forward with the urging of those around her. She took a deep breath. No words came out. She had too many thoughts, they jammed.

Sayer: Cheryl, you are worrying far too much lately. Relationships require relating. Let your wishes be known and then forget them. Stop brooding over interpersonal relationships or the lack thereof. Focus on your life goals. Want less and you will find yourself less wanting. Cheryl, does that make sense to you?

Cheryl Hunt: Yes, it does. Perfect sense. How could you know? And I'm sure you're right. I have to learn to tell people what I want and not worry so much about it. Thank you. Thank you very much.

Cheryl went back to her seat like a child leaving Santa Claus with assurances of gifts to come.

The next name Sayer called was John Cole-Parker. The man who stood up had a just-manicured look in his designer sweats—dry as talc—and gold watch. This was the same man who had originally greeted Pat and Willy wearing a three-piece suit. He could change his clothes but not his cloth—smooth as silk.

John Cole-Parker: Sayer, my interdimensional wisdom broker, I am truly happy to speak with you. You know, of course, that I'm about to open another Motivational Center, this one in Houston. This means that I'll be back on the lecture circuit. I have a new line of subliminal tapes I'm going to market. Busy, busy, busy. Oh, I'm sure it will be a great success, but... I'd like very much to know what you think.

Sayer: Stop for a moment and ask yourself why it is you strive. Do not confuse *the goal* with *the purpose*. The evolution achieved along the path is life itself. A path too strictly adhered to is itself a barrier. Roads must branch. If you are to truly motivate others, you will delegate much of the work ahead. There is someone close to you who would be valuable if given the opportunity. And John, do not overlook the physical plane. Enjoy the fruits of your labor. See to your health. Remember the lessons of past lives. John, does that make sense to you?

John Cole-Parker: Yes... it does. I've been thinking along those lines lately, and that was exactly what I needed to hear. I know just who you're talking about, too. Thank you, Sayer. I'm going to take your advice... first thing Monday morning.

Sayer went on in this fortune cookie fashion for forty-five minutes. Greta explained that she schedules a private session with Aunt Dorethea during the week. For this, a donation, usually between fifty and a hundred, is recommended. The private session reveals more personal insights in far greater detail. The group meetings are more of a social function.

Sayer's creaky humming once again preceded the next name, opening the interdimensional door: "Willy Freeman."

Now wait one minute—Willy's mind was calling for a time-out. *What the fuck's going on? Did she say my name?*

"Willy Freeman," she said it again.

Propped up by Greta and Pat, he found himself standing there like an understudy in a school play.

Sayer: Willy Freeman, tell us by what other name you are to be known.

Willy: You mean *Spokes?*

Sayer: Spokes, indeed. It is not often I come across a young man such as this—an old soul, a fifth-level king in the reflective mode with a goal of ascendancy. Both skeptic and believer in one—do not be impatient. It is no accident that you have come here to this house at this particular time, the ascending sign on the eastern horizon. It is time for you to re-examine your old inner/outer and self/other designations. There are two ways of entering this world; one of them is through the female body. Spokes, does that make sense to you?

Make sense? Willy was completely baffled to say the least. He had no idea what the fuck she-he-it was talking about. He didn't know what kind of game she was running—maybe all that garbage was supposed to impress him. Everyone was looking at him like he was supposed to answer back, like he knew what the fuck it all meant.

Still, he was beginning to feel less frightened, and more amused. It was really pretty amusing stuff—all this mumbo jumbo. *What the hell! Why not play along? Have a little fun!*

He leveled a long penetrating stare at Aunt Dorethea. In his mind he made sure to eyeball Aunt Dorethea and not this Sayer character. Then, he started breathing by snatches. He developed a spreading blight of tics. And when the paroxysm was finished playing upon his face, a calm settled onto his countenance and he began to percolate a creaky tuneless hum.

That was all it took—a distracted little purr; it was instantly recognizable. A gasp swept over the Gathering, draining the color from cheeks and unhinging jaws.

But the one being to become truly unhinged was Sayer. The steel will that commanded the osteoporotic spine erect faltered as Sayer crumpled back down to the dowager's hump that was Aunt Dorethea; the faraway eyes focused on the surprise package that was standing in front of her, stealing the very voice right out of her.

Spokes: Dorethea, dear dear Dorethea, this is Sayer giving guidance... to you, not through you like I usually do. I have channeled through you for a hundred years. You grow fatigued. Aunt Dorethea, dear channel, does that make sense to you...? I'm... changing... channels.

Whatever it was that possessed Willy to kid around like that with Aunt Dorethea, he was awfully sorry he'd done it. It was more than the old woman could take. She grasped at her collar, offered up a volley of weak otherworldly sounds; then, stroked out.

~~~

Chapter 17

In the great game of human life one begins by being a dupe and ends by being a rogue.

—Voltaire

It was a hop-step of a jaunt from Greta's Beverly Hills estate on Roxbury Drive to Aunt Dorethea's hospital room on the seventh floor of Cedars-Sinai. During the past three weeks Greta's Mercedes had made that shuttle so many times that there was actually more than one occasion when Greta was headed elsewhere and automatically steered to Beverly Boulevard, along the hospital route.

How gracious to have Willy and Pat stay at the guest house! A two-story stone structure in the same stately style as the main house, it stood surrounded by painstakingly tended shrubs. A series of terraces led around the big house, through the garden, and alongside the pool. Offerings of statuary highlighted the grounds. A statue of Buddha sat incongruously in the rose garden. Given Willy's newfound status as medium to the spirit guide and teacher known as Sayer, it was unclear if it was Greta who was being gracious, or Willy. Probably Willy.

Though the guest house had all the amenities one could want, Greta made a point to tell Willy that he had the run of the big house as well. That went especially for the library which Greta had compiled as a sort of shrine to the studies of the Atlantis Fellowship, and to the entity known as Sayer. It contained countless transcripts of sessions with Aunt Dorethea along with video and audio tapes. Over the years Greta had become Aunt Dorethea's self-appointed archivist. There were walls of mahogany bookshelves lined with texts covering all manner of metaphysics: astrology, numerology, tarot, palmistry, astral projection, reincarnation. There were books on the Lost City of Atlantis. There was even a section devoted to witchcraft and sorcery.

It was probably one of the best privately owned such collections. And yet there was nothing in any of those books that could help the beloved Dorethea. The doctors didn't hold out much hope for her recovery. It had taken too long to get her from the desert to the hospital; and even so, it might not have made a difference. A massive cerebral vascular accident was what they called it. Somewhere in that wise and clever little grey head a blood vessel had burst, depriving her brain of oxygen. A CAT scan revealed that the area controlling movements of the tongue, lips, and vocal cords was ischemic; in other words, they would not be hearing any more from Aunt Dorethea. Pity. Willy was just beginning to realize how incredibly wily the old broad really was.

Old or young, women were a mystery. And Willy was still at

that point in life where it was all he could do to try to understand himself. Women were another species altogether. Even Pat. She had been acting different lately, growing distant. She spent time going for long walks. She would take the van and disappear for the whole day. He shrugged it off—female moodiness.

So with Greta at the hospital and Pat off by herself, Willy became increasingly absorbed in Greta's library. There, among the charts and incantations, his respect for Aunt Dorethea grew. The way he saw it, she had one incredible racket going on.

A couple of weeks went by and Willy started to notice something. Phone calls were coming in. Only a few at first. People didn't want to seem somehow disrespectful, but they wanted to know if Spokes—most of them called him Spokes—was going to hold private audiences. Aunt Dorethea or not, life went on. They needed to speak with their guide and spirit teacher.

At first Willy had feared that he would be blamed for what happened. In the desert he had waited among the stunned and grieving followers of the fallen oracle for someone to denounce him. But there was to be no condemnation. After all, she was a very old woman and he was only a boy. The Harmonic Convergence, as promised, had delivered a miracle.

The phone in the study rang. The answering machine clicked and the red *in use* light went on. Willy listened in as the caller, Bruce Wilson, told Greta that the regular monthly meeting—*had it really been a month?*—was going to take place at Sharon Markham's home. Everyone was going to get together to meditate and offer prayer for Aunt Dorethea's recovery. *Click—* end of message.

It wasn't eavesdropping. Not really. Eavesdropping had a degree of prurient pleasure associated with it. A titillating sensation. And it was the sensation of eavesdropping that compelled young Willy to the library. Here were endless revelations concerning the most private aspects of the lives of the members of the Atlantis Fellowship. Secrets not easily relinquished to clergyman or doctor were readily divulged to Sayer.

"I'm home," Greta called out as though she were speaking to the house—not Carmen, the Spanish-speaking maid; not the curious young houseguest holed up in the library—but to the house itself.

The time had come. Willy had loaded up on enough ammunition; now he was going to have to surface and try a little target practice. He cleared his throat and went to meet Greta.

"Oh!... Willy, dear, you startled me."

"I'm sorry. I didn't mean to—"

"I know you didn't," Greta said to Willy. It hadn't registered. She went on, "I don't know what's wrong with me. Lately I'm so—"

Greta was carrying a shopping bag from Nordstrom; she dropped it in the middle of the floor. Even her rouge blanched. It dawned on her—*that had been the voice of Aunt Dorethea standing before her in jeans and a T-shirt.*

"Greta... my sister—you know we were sisters in another

life, don't you?—I'm sorry I didn't confide in you more... while on the earthly plane. But sisters can be so jealous.... Do you forgive me?"

Greta the Gregarious stood struggling for words. "Dorethea... there's nothing to forgive. I adored you... always. Please... where are you?"

Willy's eyes maintained an unseeing inward stare while his face bubbled over with the shunting of spirits. "She is safe... with me," said Sayer.

If he could fool Greta, he could fool any of them. They spoke for nearly an hour and he was amazed at how eager she was to believe. When he got stuck on a detail, she would bail him out with the missing particulars. If he inadvertently contradicted himself, she was ready with some convoluted logic to explain it away.

By the time the trance was broken and the here and now was once again turned over to a worn-out, seemingly mystified Spokes, Greta had agreed to accompany Willy to the meeting. She could not have been more thrilled with her ward.

For Willy, it was all beginning to gel. A plan was coming together. He was bursting with excitement and needed someone to share it with. *Where was Pat?*

The sky was everything a sky is supposed to be. The sunlight bounced off the ocean like hundreds of mirrors signaling to the mountains that stood nearby. Mountains and sea sharing the same line of sight, and people everywhere she looked. So many people. Pat squinted at the scene that was Venice Beach. She was taking in the sights like a camera, very aware that she would most definitely tell people back home what she'd seen, what she was seeing. She didn't think about it, but she was smiling. Practically grinning. It was stuck to her face and wouldn't come off. What a find! Ocean Front Walk. She was in her element. Different but the same. The sights, the smells, the sounds—to Pat it felt like an infusion of life. She bopped around, weaving her way through crowds. Everything vying for attention. Stalls lined the route— posters, sunglasses, T-shirts. Sidewalk cafes. And ah yes!—street performers. Don't forget street performers! It was all there. Humanity's bazaar—and how!

On top of all this, something wonderful happened. It really wasn't any big deal but that didn't make it any less wonderful. Someone riding by on a bicycle said "Hello Pat." She didn't know him. The face was vaguely familiar. But he knew her. And he slowed down long enough to say hello and to ask, "Where's your guitar?" Three thousand miles from Bleecker Street and she got recognized.

When Pat got back to the guest house it was almost dark. She was walking like it was a new morning. She was singing, the clear bell of her voice at the door.

"Where've you been?" were the first words out of Willy's mouth.

Pat looked at him sideways. "If you gimme a chance, I might even tell you."

"It doesn't matter. Wait till you hear what I did."

A blind man would have seen the shadow cross Pat's face. But not Willy. He was too caught up in his own little intrigue. Pat listened sullenly as he told her of the artful sham he put over on Greta, and of his scheme for the Fellowship.

They didn't do it that night; Pat wasn't in the mood.

Willy was beginning to think women were more trouble than they were worth.

Neither one of them slept well and when Sunday morning shined down on them, they didn't shine back.

Willy got out of bed first. Rosey had been in his dreams. It was something about Rosey being his big brother; and the next minute, he, himself, was Rosey. It's wild the way dreams don't need to adhere to any consistency.

He checked the time. Took a shower. Checked the time again.

Pat always awoke a little grumpy; Willy didn't notice anything different. She put up coffee. He was preoccupied with himself, more than usual. He was feeling like a student on the day of a big exam.

They drove the 101 out to Encino in silence—Greta, Pat, and Willy. Willy sat in the back by himself. It made him feel like a VIP. He imagined he was in a limo. From the backseat of a Mercedes 450 SEL, it didn't take much imagination.

The Markhams' house was built in a style that seemed to

apologize for its enormity. It had the modest look of Small Town, U.S.A. Only it had sixteen bedrooms and sat astride a hilltop south of the boulevard.

There was no room to park in the circular driveway, or for a block in either direction. Greta wasn't one to arrive early. She knew that in order to make a proper entrance, you must have a full reception. So it was that they walked a short distance. Hand in hand they approached the front door. Greta linked arms with Willy, behaving positively possessive. He, in turn, reached to take Pat's hand; she grudgingly acquiesced. The door opened before the doorbell could complete its chiming and they were sucked in.

On Greta's coattails they had to endure as she attempted to greet one and all. Half-hugs and air kisses flew. And all the while she kept an eye on Willy to make sure he stayed close. People made a point to say hello to Willy, and to Pat. They all knew his name, and hers: "Hello, Willy. Hello, Pat." Some said, "Hello, Spokes." They were trying very hard to make them feel welcome. It felt... not natural. Pat screwed her face into a look of disapproval. She felt out of place.

Willy was otherwise engaged. As people came up to him and introduced themselves, as each face and name registered before him, so too did a corresponding dossier of personal information pop up, gleaned from Greta's library. He had prepared well.

He was careful not to say much; he would say "Hello, pleased to meet you," and he would think, *All in good time.*

~~~

Chapter 18

If the world will be gulled, let it be gulled.

—*Robert Burton*

It had been a week since the "revelations" of the Fellowship meeting at the Markham house, and Pat was having a hard time with it. She didn't say anything to anyone. It wasn't her place to be telling the party-goers that the debutante wore falsies.

It was beginning to feel like there was no place for her in California. And to prove the point, she was having a hard time finding a parking space. She drove around in circles, all around Venice Beach. Finally she gave up and parked in a lot. Five bucks—what a rip off! She never had that problem in New York. Of course, she never drove in New York.

It was a carbon copy beautiful day. The to and fro along Ocean Front Walk bustled with the beat of a windup toy, only it failed to work its magic. The child's eye within the woman didn't sparkle in wonderment. Not today. Not the piano player, not the jugglers, not the clown with the purple wig, not the roller-skate dancers, not the muscle men, not unicycles, not tandem bicycles—no one and nothing could clear her troubled mind. A

173

monarch butterfly floated past, unnoticed.

A fat lady in a muumuu, engulfing a defenseless folding chair, looked up at Pat. Beside her, on a diminutive card table was a sign:

SPIRITUAL READINGS

PAST-PRESENT-FUTURE

DONATIONS ACCEPTED

This, Pat noticed.

A chair on the other side of the table sat empty waiting for a customer.

Pat put down her guitar case, thought about opening it—it was as good a spot as any—then changed her mind.

"Well, aren't you going to play?" the fortuneteller inquired. "I like to listen... and besides, it brings people 'round."

Pat gave her a short snort. Whenever Pat felt troubled, as she did now, she would invariably come across as defiant. "Are you a phony, too?" she asked.

"Too...?" said the fortuneteller. "If you're not going to play... Why not have a seat?" she motioned to the empty chair. Then, reading the hesitation in Pat's body language, she really did read her mind: "Oh, don't worry! This one's on the house.... You're a fellow street artist. Consider it a professional courtesy."

With that, Pat lowered herself into the chair—like getting into hot water.

But after they'd settled into a conversation—like a hot bath—it started to relax her.

The beauty of the fortuneteller's art is simple: the customer gets what she wants. That is, she gets to talk about her favorite subject—herself. As she talks she reveals more and more. Soon it becomes clear what it is she wants to hear. Most of the time she wants to hear that her future has good things in store. So she's told good things and she leaves happy. What could be simpler!

But Pat proved to be frustrating. For one thing, she had no interest in hearing about herself. The fortuneteller pretended to look at her palm and ascertained that Pat had endured a difficult life. She only glanced at the palm while studying the eyes. Pat was visibly unimpressed.

"All I want to know is what's going to happen to this friend of mine."

The fortuneteller honed in: "You're troubled about a friend.... Am I right? This... friend, he is your boyfriend...? but you broke up...? Am I right?"

Pat didn't have patience for this; she needed someone she could talk to.

So Pat told the fortuneteller about "this friend" of hers who was perpetrating a terrible fraud, or as she put it, "...makin' believe he's somethin' he ain't... and foolin' a whole lotta people." She went on to say that she knew it was wrong... what he was doing, but that she didn't think it proper to be tellin' a grownup his wrong from right. She was facing a moral dilemma.

And there was something else; another question was bothering her. As Pat so eloquently put it, she, herself, didn't get no school past the eighth grade, but she wanted to know "How come people that's supposed to be educated... are so quick to be fooled into believin' things that ain't true?"

It was a good question and it deserved an answer. But the fortuneteller wasn't up to it. So she went with the old standby; she said, "Dear, I want you to make a wish. Think about this person... and make a wish. Here, give me your hand." She fished something out of her pocket and put it in Pat's hand. It looked like some kind of acorn. "That's a special seed," she said. "I said very special prayers over that seed. It's the seed of an idea from out of which your wish can grow. You must take that seed and throw it in the ocean and your wish will come true." She said it with matter-of-fact certainty.

Pat bounced a look from the fortuneteller to the acorn to the shimmering blue that lay just beyond the sand.

As Pat started to get up, the fortuneteller quickly added, "It'll be $3 for the seed."

Pat stopped halfway between sitting and standing. Hesitating, she said, "I'll give you a buck. Take it or leave it."

"...I'll take it."

Pat gave her the dollar; the fortuneteller gave her her blessing. Clutching the acorn tightly, Pat walked toward the water's edge. Funny, it suddenly struck her that here, all along, she'd been coming to the beach, but she hadn't yet been to the water. A group of seagulls burrowed their bottoms in the soft sand. They didn't fly when Pat walked past, which surprised her. One very white gull with just traces of grey stood on his bird legs and lifted into the sky, gliding low over the sand for a few hundred feet before settling back down. Near the water a large encrusted drainpipe lay exposed from beneath the sand. It ran down from the city sewers like a mutant river to the sea. Incredibly quick little birds stepped around piles of washed up seaweed, broken shells, and bits of refuse: a bottle top here, a plastic cup there. The pipe disappeared into a jetty of rocks. The jetties separated the beach inlets which looped around in a serrated shore. Down the beach a ways Pat could see a pier sticking out in the water, like an unfinished bridge. And when she squinted out across the ocean she tried to imagine China.

Her thoughts got lost in the ceaseless roll of the waves.

Three surfers bobbed on the surface. Then a fourth paddled out to join them. From a seat on the rocks, she watched them ride the waves.

For a moment she forgot all about the hard little seed in her hand. She rolled it in her palm.

No, she couldn't get it out of her mind: the scene at the Markham house; the way all those rich people looked at Willy when he made believe he was that poor lady, Aunt Dorethea; and then, that he was their guide and spirit teacher, Sayer. They believed him. Like they were in church or something. She knew it wasn't right—turning a nightclub act into a miracle. All those people, treating him like he was the Pope. He was Willy, not some spiritual leader calling himself Spokes. She wanted her lover boy back.

She stood up on the jetty and flung her arm wide. The seed arced, and for a moment it seemed to hang in the wind. But it never made it to the water. It never fell back down to earth. A great big seagull swooped it out of the air and flew away with it in his beak.

~~~

Chapter 19

Fame and admiration weigh not a feather in the scale against friendship and love...

—*George Sand*

"Greta...? Have you seen Pat?" Spokes called out across the garden.

He finally had a free moment to himself. Ever since the Markham house his calendar was booked solid with people wanting to get in to talk to Sayer.

Greta was in heaven. She had long coveted the position of personal secretary to Aunt Dorethea, a position formerly held by Bruce Wilson; and now, through what could only be termed a miracle, it had come to pass. And she approached her new job with great zeal. Things were happening so fast. That day, she had scheduled a *People Magazine* interview. Later that afternoon they were due at NBC Studios to tape a segment for "The Donahue Show." Greta saw the suddenness with which Spokes was thrust into the limelight as being part of the miracle, gathering momentum, the spreading light.

Those in the news media had a somewhat different

viewpoint: it was a slow news week; they had geared up for this New Age nonevent called the Harmonic Convergence and now they needed an angle; the Atlantis Fellowship had several well-placed people in the media; and the story of Spokes, the fifteen year old channeler, made good copy. The right place at the right time.

Greta was at the beck and call of the young master. "Pat...? Yes, she was here, fifteen minutes ago. Said she wanted to talk to you. But you were with Mr. Cole-Parker. I didn't want to disturb the session. She said she was just going for a walk and she'd be right back.... That's what she said."

Just then the door bell rang.

Speaking of the devil, they could hear Pat's voice clear out in the garden. They could hear Carmen, the maid, was yammering away in Spanish. And there was another voice—a male voice—trying to be heard above the fracas.

Spokes sprang up to go see what was going on. Greta followed close behind, through the lush garden, over the plush carpet, to the grand vestibule. Just inside the double doors, beneath the chandelier at the foot of the winding staircase, short black Pat from Harlem stood clenching her jaw and flaring her nostrils at a tall white Beverly Hills policeman.

He directed his attention to Greta. "Pardon me, Ma'am, sorry to trouble you. The young lady says she's a houseguest here?"

"Yes, Officer, that's correct. Is there any problem?"

"No, there's no problem." He was being very polite.

Speaking to Pat he added, "Miss, sorry if you were inconvenienced in any way. I'm sure, if you think about it, you'll see it's for your own protection; you really should carry ID."

Despite the apparent disparagement in height, Pat managed to look down her nose at him.

He smiled, letting her animosity wash over him, and bowing out, he bid everyone "You have a pleasant day now."

"Good day to you, Officer," Greta returned, closing the tall oak door behind.

You had to say one thing for Pat: she put on a brave face. But when the door shut, and the perceived threat was no longer present, she let go. The clenched jaw trembled, the stone face wrinkled, and the damn-you-to-hell eyes burst out in tears.

"Oh my! How dreadful!" Greta was instantly empathetic. "Now dear, you mustn't cry. That stupid man's not worth spoiling your pretty face over."

Between spasmodic gasps of breath, Pat threw a garbled string of words at Greta that Greta couldn't quite make out. "Who you kidding? You don't think I'm pretty." Then she ran away to the guest house.

Greta looked to Spokes. He had understood what Pat said. She said that wasn't why she was crying; she said Greta was an old fool.

"You'd better go see if she's alright, the poor dear," suggested Greta. "But Spokes," she cautioned, "please, be quick about it. We have to leave for the studio," she glanced at her diamond wristwatch, "...very soon."

181

By time he caught up with Pat, the tears were under control. She sat in front of a mirror, applying resolved; self-indulgence wasn't a part of her makeup.

"I'm going back to New York" were the first words out of her mouth.

"Now why would you want to do that? Especially now... when everything's going so good."

She looked past herself. Her eyes were great big pools of love and the tears. He could see himself in their reflection. "I don't belong here... and neither do you."

"What are you saying? Just 'cause of some cop? They're not used to seeing black people walking around here, that's all. You're safer here than... riding the *A* train." He knew that would hit a nerve.

"You jus' don't understand, do you? I don't give a fuck about that cop. You... you the one I—" She closed her eyes.

"What? Finish what you're saying. I'm the one you... What?"

"I worry for you, Willy. It's not right, what you're doing. I don't want to see it. But I'm not going to interfere. I'm going home." When she finished saying that, she opened her eyes, looked at him, and said, "Come back with me?"

A soft knocking at the door pushed aside the question. Greta spoke through the door, hastening, "Spokes, it's time. We have to leave... now."

"Listen, Pat, we'll talk about this later. I have to go."

He went to give her a soft closed-mouth kiss on the lips. She suddenly reached up and passionately pulled his mouth onto hers, for a long, deep taste of her lover boy. When she released him, he was reeling and bemused.

Galloping down the stairs to the waiting Mercedes, he called back, "I'm going to be on 'The Donahue Show'."

Pat knew if she was going to do it, she had to do it right away—it wasn't going to get easier.

She slid a folded piece of paper out of the front pocket of her tight jeans. Laying it flat next to the phone, sand spilled from the folds. She read the number as she dialed *859-4613*.

"Hello, taxi service? ...I need a cab to the airport."

~~~

Chapter 20

When you got money, you got lots of friends crowding round your door.

—*Billie Holiday*

Carmen back stepped with surprising agility as she attempted to bar the way to the uninvited visitor. She was about as effective as a flyswatter on a wolf. Which was precisely who the gate-crasher turned out to be—none other than Wolfee.

"Spokes, my man, I see you're up to your old tricks, impersonating someone you ain't.... Don't just sit there with your mouth open, tell the señorita here to bring your old friend Wolfee a cold drink."

Upon seeing Wolfee he reacted like he was truly possessed. He sat straight up and shook his head and rubbed his eyes, as if he were trying to rid himself of an apparition.

"Well...?" Wolfee growled impatiently. He grabbed Spokes by the front of the shirt and lifted him out of the chaise lounge. "Whatsa matter? You lose your voice...? All thousand of 'em? You better find one of 'em fast, and tell old Wolfee how glad you are to see him."

Wolfee definitely bore the mark of the nutjob: he could

change moods from "buddy-buddy" one minute to mad dog the next. It was truly scary.

Spokes effected a quick change of his own, instantly adopting the guise of conviviality: "Wolfee, glad to see you. Relax. Have a seat. You've come a long way...."

From listening to Carmen and Greta, Spokes had picked up a few words of Spanish, enough to say, "Carmen, esta bien.... Una cerveza por Señor Wolfee, por favor."

Carmen retreated to the kitchen to get the beer. Spokes was glad she didn't understand much English. He was glad that Greta wasn't home. He turned to Wolfee. "Wolfee, you mustn't let anybody hear you say stuff like that, ever."

"Like what?" Wolfee could grin with the best of them.

"You know... that stuff about me doing voices, impersonating who I ain't."

In a strange sort of way, it was a relief to see Wolfee. Ever since Pat left, Spokes had been feeling terribly disconnected. She left him a note that warned "...No good can come from this *Sayer* business." Not that he put any faith in that karma crap... but Pat had been the only person who knew he was a phony; she shared his secret.

And now there was Wolfee.

"Yeah... I know all about it. I caught your... your performance on 'Donahue'."

The media had dubbed Spokes *The Fifteen Year Old Mystic*.

Spoker, for a little guy, you got balls—" Wolfee shut up when he saw Carmen returning.

185

Carmen set the tray down next to him and poured the beer into a glass. Then she turned quickly to go—but not quickly enough. Wolfee gave her a good smack on her well-padded bottom. She let out an excited little yelp and stamped her foot like a flamenco dancer, then tucked her butt in and made a getaway on short fast steps.

Wolfee's eyes followed after her. "Not only is that built for comfort, it can move." Wolfee turned back to Spokes. "Spokes, my man, I'm gonna like it here."

An electronic pulpit preacher once remarked on how the modern miracle of television had the power to send the message of Christ to more people in a minute than Jesus himself could have reached in His entire lifetime. Whether this observation bears testimony to the enduring strength of a 2000 year old message delivered via so humble a means or to the paltry content cluttering our present-day airwaves, Spokes' 15 minutes of fame brought forth more than his share of disciples, hangers-on, and just plain nuisances. After several appearances on the tube, he had queries from psychic researchers, fan mail from satanic cults, and obscenely hateful phone calls from evangelical fundamentalists. As it turned out, Wolfee actually earned his keep. In keeping with Spokes' growing celebrity, it seemed only fitting that he should have a bodyguard. The official designation as Spokes' Chief of Security fell quite naturally onto those broad shoulders.

＊ ＊ ＊ ＊ ＊

Several days after Wolfee's arrival, Spokes, along with a small entourage—nine people traveling in three cars—went for a spin to a psychic fair in Pasadena. The weekend freeway wasn't at all crowded; zipping along through the smog, there was the distinct feeling of being on holiday—a busman's holiday—even if only for the afternoon. Spokes needed to get away. Business was *that* good. Money, power, all kinds of offers—it was all pouring in. Everyone wanted an audience with the Fifteen Year Old Mystic.

They arrived at the fair and it didn't take long for Spokes to conclude that the exhibits were of little interest. It had been Greta's idea to come to the fair. The promoters were friends of hers and they had sent complimentary tickets. In psychic circles, Spokes was already renowned. No doubt the Fifteen Year Old Mystic would prove a windfall draw to any such fair. *A ridiculous notion!* Such pedestrian marketing would be totally inappropriate for his clientele. After giving the place the once-over, the expedition grouped back out in the parking lot.

It was there, in the parking lot, that Wolfee unequivocally established himself as Spokes' Chief of Security. A strange man approached. He was so tall, it was as if he were standing on a soapbox. His clothes and his face looked wooden; only his eyes were polished with liquid fire, the same as the burnish coming off the heavy silver crucifix that he clutched to his chest. Oddly enough, no one noticed him until he was practically on top of

Spokes, shouting "Death to the anti-Christ."

Spokes and his entourage experienced a simultaneous panic which coursed from their stomachs to their feet. And they froze.

All except for Wolfee. Wolfee stepped up to the man and peacefully punched him in the stomach. *Peacefully punched* may seem like a contradiction in terms. Even so, Wolfee was so calm that it did seem perfectly peaceful. The threat that had stood before them doubled over, then crumpled to his knees.

They went on to their cars as if nothing had happened.

But something had happened—and it was the highlight of the outing; and perhaps, for some time to come. They had something to talk about: how there had been an attempt on the life of the Fifteen Year Old Mystic and how his magnificent bodyguard had intervened. There would be questions as to whether or not the assailant had a knife or a gun. And there would be wonderment at the magnanimous nature of the transcendent boy who let his would-be assassin go free rather than hand him over to the authorities: *To forgive is divine.* Ultimately, the episode served to exaggerate the status of the young avatar and his followers. And Wolfee... he now had a reputation as a tough guy that went from coast-to-coast.

In the days that followed, Greta took Wolfee to Rodeo Drive. If he was going to be their Chief of Security, he needed to look the part. Despite her best effort, he still came away with a dozen of the most garish shirts he could find. She did manage eventually to talk him into several Armani suits.

After their shopping spree, Wolfee took himself on a

different kind of shopping expedition—to a gun shop where he purchased a snub-nose 38. and a shoulder holster, to go with his new suits. But generally, he preferred to carry the piece tucked under his waistband at the small of his back.

All in all, he was a very happy thug. He was finally getting his piece of the action.

An amusing epilogue: If anyone had stuck around that parking lot, they'd have seen that same strange man approaching any and all visitors to the psychic fair. Once he recovered from his bellyache, he was back at it, same as before. "Death to the anti-Christ" was his theme for the day; truth was, he didn't know Spokes from Adam.

Dinner at the Gilmore residence had taken on a whole new dimension since the coming of Spokes. Before, it had been too lonely to set a place in the grand dining hall. Now, there always seemed to be visitors seated the length of the table. Every meal had the flavor of an occasion. It was as though you half expected the scene to someday be reproduced in a painting. Spokes' place was at the head of the table; Greta, to one side; Wolfee, at the other.

For the first time in a long time, since the night Rosey died, Spokes let himself think that everything was going to be alright. It was as if his soul had been convalescing and he was just now beginning to get back his appetite. The gnawing guilt was rendered temporarily toothless, the knots of fear relaxed, the yammering of conscience was hushed by the insulation of money. He had no time for ghosts; the company of devotees, a lavish banquet—he was too full of exaltation and good food, and of course, fine spirits.

Prime rib was Wolfee's favorite, and this was the best he'd ever tasted. As Carmen cleared the table, Spokes noticed that she winked at Wolfee. No one was supposed to see, but it was too late now. No one was supposed to know, but it was obvious—the way she acted when she was around Wolfee. Spokes wasn't the only one at the table who had noticed. The cat was out of the bag. Wolfee looked over at Spokes from under his brow. He had that look like he was going to burp canary feathers any minute. He smacked his lips making a long loud squeegee sound. Carmen blushed as she hurried into the kitchen.

"Well, whadaya know! " Spokes grinned. "And all this time I thought she couldn't stand you. From here on, ain't nothing surprises me anymore."

There was a knock at the front door. Greta said to no one in particular, "Are you expecting anyone?" When no one answered she said, "Wolfee, dear, would you be good enough to see who that is...?"

A moment later Wolfee returned. He was holding two suitcases, one by the handle and one under the arm. A *jingle-jangle*, like a jailer's hefty key ring, was following him. Whoever was keeping pace behind him was too small to see, hidden by the broadness of the bodyguard turned porter.

"Hey, Spokes, look who's here! It's your—" Wolfee stepped aside and—

Helene Freeman smiled like a jack-o-lantern. "Surprise!"

"Mother!"

~~~

Chapter 21

If your lips would keep from slips
Five things observe with care:
To whom you speak, of whom you speak,
And how, and when, and where.

—Anonymous

Click click. The man slouching in the Ford LTD Crown Vic used a telescopic lens; he took pictures of Wolfee when he came to answer the door.

The cabbie was getting back into his cab. He pushed the heel of his hand into his low back; he talked to himself, "Goddamn suitcases! *Uuuuh!* My aching back!" With a twist and a stretch, he looked over his shoulder to the blue Ford parked curbside. Someone was watching him from inside that car. The cabbie went right on talking to himself. "If you're going to be inconspicuous in this neighborhood, you better get a Mercedes." Then telling himself it was none of his business, he put the cab in drive and slowly drove away.

The man in the Ford snapped a parting shot of the taxi's plates.

He was an odd looking shutterbug: clean-cut, definitely not an artist; wore a tie, not a tourist. He was no newsman although some of his co-workers at the field office had taken to calling him Jimmy Olsen, as in Jimmy Olsen, Cub Reporter. His last name was Olsen, but his first name wasn't Jimmy, and he didn't much care for the nickname. But he was stuck with it. And all because he had the misfortune to be working with an agent named Clark. His last name wasn't Kent. Not that that mattered. They were Clark and Olsen.

Olsen said, "Get a load of the guy who answered the door."

Clark didn't take his eyes off the house. He took off his glasses and peered through a small pair of high-tech field glasses. His mouth gave a twitch at the corners, which was tantamount to a smile. He had a way about him: whatever he said sounded like *I told you so*. His answer to Olsen: "Not your typical Beverly Hills butler."

Several hours past. Greta's dinner guests left. There were no more cars in the driveway. Olsen went through two rolls of film. And the whole time, the two men didn't say a word. Occupational hazard—when you're in the snooping business you learn not to talk too much.

There are no trash cans on the sidewalks in Beverly Hills. Behind all the houses there are immaculate service roads. Each house has its own dumpster. These are oversized containers molded of thick green rubber; the City of Beverly Hills has their own specially equipped garbage trucks to handle their special dumpsters. The lids are hinged in the middle so they open like the gull-wing doors of a 1954 Mercedes sports car.

In the 6 AM sky, as the night was still receding, the morning haze loitered in the service road. Not even the birds were up. A shopping cart laden with cans and bottles abutted the rear wall of the Gilmore residence while the person belonging to the cart rummaged inside the dumpster. A street person going through garbage—nothing that unusual. This was, by all standards, very select garbage. And this was apparently a very selective scrounge. He was only going through that particular garbage can. Something else peculiar about him—he had a fresh haircut.

Olsen, in his new role as garbage picker, climbed out of the dumpster. Pushing his cart, he grumbled to himself just like a real street person: "Why do I always get the stinky jobs? He gets to run a wiretap. I get to sift through a pile of leftover crap..."

Further down the block, he linked up with his partner. Clark was at one of those large green telephone company boxes. They're scattered throughout the city, just another feature on the urban landscape. A panel truck with the Pacific Bell orange logo was parked alongside this one. He wore one of those tool belts with a handset clipped on. Just a telephone company worker on a service call.

A telephone company worker having a conversation with a rag picker.

"Well, anything?"

"Nothing. Garbage. Just garbage."

"Okay... Go get cleaned up. You stink! And bring back some

coffee... maybe some McMuffins or something. We're going to be here a while." Clark turned his back as if disgusted by the other man's filth. He resumed messing with the wires.

Olsen abandoned the cart and shuffled off looking dejected, still muttering to himself: "It's gonna be a long day..."

It wasn't until late morning, early afternoon, that the line came alive with chatter. Greta the Gregarious, hard at work getting out the gossip.

In the back of the phone company van, the eavesdroppers sat, headsets to their ears, her most attentive audience. The two men listened in like biddies glued to their favorite soap opera. A tape recorder was reeling it all in.

Greta was having a hard time coming to terms with Mrs. Freeman. Here was the mother of the person who, as far as Greta was concerned, was the embodiment of the New Age movement... and she ends up being an embarrassment.

"She's as coarse as they come and full of moxie. She's here less than fifteen minutes and she's trying to sell me this wretched jewelry that she brought from Mexico.... Can you believe it!... I was so embarrassed for Spokes that I bought a bracelet... No, that's what she does... for a living!... I think she said—now don't quote me on this—that she's a part-time travel agent... and she sells trinkets to housewives in Brooklyn.... Two big suitcases full... No, I didn't ask... I wouldn't put it past her... She wears enough to fill a third suitcase... No, not like that... cheap bracelets, necklaces... You should have seen... Second thought, you're better off... No, thank goodness... just a stopover to see her 'Willy'... Back to New York... this evening... LAX."

This same conversation was repeated half a dozen times. Minor changes, but essentially the same.

Interspersed with these calls were several others in which Greta was busy apologizing as she cancelled Spokes' appointments; he wanted to spend the day with his mother. She rescheduled these. And then there were about a dozen calls from people wanting to schedule private sessions with Sayer. There was currently a six week wait. She handled it all very efficiently.

This was turning out to be dreadfully boring. If anyone happened by the Pac Bell truck—not that anyone did—they'd take for granted that it was a couple of workers asleep on the job. They could have picked a better place to goof off. The sun was baking down on the roof. Olsen looked very unhappy. His face was getting blotchy, like a colicky baby. He could hear splashing coming from a nearby pool. But the thing that burned him up the most was Clark—always so cool and collected.

Then finally, a call came in that seemed like it might be something. Clark, who was already sitting up, sat up even straighter. It was about three in the afternoon, long distance from New York. Someone wanted to speak to Helene Freeman.

"And who shall I say is calling?" Greta inquired. Naturally, she was dying to know.

She wasn't the only one.

"And who is this?" the caller asked back.

Greta was taken slightly aback by this; you could hear it as she answered, "Why!... this is Greta Gilmore."

"Tell Helene it's Jimmy... Jimmy in New York."

"Hold one minute, Jimmy. I'll see if I can locate her."

Jimmy waited.

The men in the Pac Bell truck waited.

Helene was out by the pool playing cards with her son and Wolfee. Carmen scurried forward with the phone. Wolfee had been teaching her English, or to be more accurate, Brooklynese. At least that was the pretense he gave for spending so much time in her room. In her thick Spanish accent Carmen repeated Greta's words: "For Mrs. Freeman. From New York. A Mr. Jimmy."

Helene allowed a tinge of surprise to cross her brow as she took the phone. "Jimmy, I was just going to call you."

There was hesitation on the other end of the line, then Jimmy said, "Okay Greta, thank you... Greta, you can hang up the phone now."

There was a *click*. Now he'd talk.

"Little girl, where the fuck were you? You was supposed to be back in New York yesterday."

"I'm sorry, James. I stopped off in LA to visit with my son." She smiled at Willy. "I decided it was something I just had to do... Why do you sound so angry?"

It was either the sweetness in her voice or more likely the genuine innocence in what she said that managed to calm his Sicilian temper.

"I'm sorry, little girl," Malfieri said. "I guess I was just

197

worried when you weren't home and you was supposed to be. I want you should come back right—"

"You're such a sweetheart. You must've been really worried... to take the trouble and find out where I was. I'm sorry I didn't call. It's just been so exciting... seeing Willy and all.... There must be something about California that makes people flaky." She threw in a laugh, it sounded forced; she was trying hard for him to lighten up. "Don't worry, Jimmy. I'm going to be leaving tonight. I'll be there tomorrow. Everything is just fine. It's been a wonderful trip..."

"And your... your business... it went good?"

"It went very well. The best buys ever! I don't know how you do these things, but—"

"I went to a lotta trouble arranging to have my friend Carlos get you a special wholesale price on them bracelets a' yours."

"You are amazing, Jimmy Malfieri. I swear, you know people all over—"

Up to now Wolfee had been sitting there playing his cards close to his chest. He suddenly realized he was holding aces and it was his call. Wolfee spoke up so loudly that Clark and Olsen both jumped to lower the volume in their headsets. "I'll say he knows people. He even knows old Wolfee. Here, gimme. Lemme say hello to my old friend, Jimmy Malfieri." He practically tore the phone out of Helene's hands. "Hey, Jimmy, my man, guess who this is?"

To Olsen and Clark it felt like a very long pause.

Wolfee got up from the table and took the phone a few feet

away. Whatever he was going to say, he didn't want anyone else to hear.

On Malfieri's end—a deadly silence. He didn't know what was going on, but he didn't like it.

As for Wolfee, he liked everything just fine. Wolfee had undergone a transformation, like in the *Wolfman*; only in this case the change was from poor dumb vicious animal into a man. Not fully upright, but a man nonetheless. This was a different, more self-assured Wolfee. It's hard to say when it first began. Perhaps it started back a hundred years ago in the project playground when Rosey challenged him and made him look small; or maybe, with a terrible promise to a doomed friend; or, with the bitter knowledge that the better man doesn't always win. Maybe it grew out of acceptance and a sense of belonging. Whatever it was, it shed his coat of self-preservation, leaving him perilously reckless.

"Ain't you even gonna say *Hello*?"

"Who is this?"

"C'mon, Jimmy... you gonna hurt my feelings. This is Wolfee. You remember Wolfee. LaPela and Bonj's friend."

"Oh, yeah... Wolfee. How you doing?"

"Okay, let's cut the crap. Listen up."

You could hear in his voice, Wolfee was having a good time calling the shots.

"Jimmy, you know what a troll is?"

"What you say?"

"A troll. You know! A troll."

"I don't know what the fuck you're talkin' about."

"Sure you do! A troll! He's a guy that lives under a bridge and when you got something you got to get across the bridge... well, you got to pay the troll."

"Now you listen, you small time piece a' shit..."

"Hey, hey! I don't have to listen to this..." Wolfee covered the phone and looked over his shoulder to Spokes and Helene. They were both staring at him. He smiled. Then, lifting the receiver to his mouth, he whispered, "Later for you, Malfieri."

And it was later for the boys on the party line as well; that was the last Clark and Olsen overheard.

Wolfee stealthily hit the disconnect, but he kept talking to the dial tone, loudly, so Helene and Spokes would hear him say, "Yeah... I'm gonna see her off to the airport... You gotta go... You want I should say goodbye to Helene for you.... Sure... I'll tell her." He hung up.

He sat back down to a curious pause. He was being viewed on the skew: *What did Wolfee have to do with Malfieri?*

He managed to break the silent inquiry by changing the subject.

"Hey, Spokes, I got an idea. We still got some time before we gotta go to the airport. Let's take your mom over to Rodeo Drive. Helene, you won't see anything like this in Brooklyn... and while we're there I'm gonna buy you the bitchinest set of Gucci luggage... so you don't have to schlep those two big suitcases to the airport.... It'll be my going-away present to you, Helene."

~~~

Chapter 22

Conscience is a mother...whose visit never ends.

—*H. L. Mencken*

There was a light rain falling as they started for the airport. It was with mixed feeling of affection and relief that Spokes saw Mom off.

Greta had made her excuse for not being able to go with them: she had a prior commitment; she was going to see a play. It turned out to be both convenient and true.

Carmen came out on the driveway to wave goodbye. Lately she was so proud, it was amusing. Her wrists jingled with the silver bracelets Wolfee had bought from Helene. Carmen was one person who was definitely glad for Mrs. Freeman's visit.

In the back of the rainbow van, a beautiful set of brand new leather suitcases jostled slightly as Wolfee, taking the turn a little sharp, bumped the rear tire over the curb as he pulled out of the driveway.

Sunset to the 405—they'd given themselves plenty of extra time, figuring on the usual delays. There was the perpetual construction slowing progress along Sunset, and the traffic around LAX was a knot in the guts of the city, guaranteed to wear equally on brakes and nerves.

It was even more frustrating keeping tabs on them: several cars behind, the Pac Bell truck played peek-a-boo amidst the flow of commuters; trying not to lose eyeshot, not to be obvious. *Follow that rainbow!*—Clark and Olsen hung tough, focused, not about to let it out of their sight.

Maybe a little too focused. As they approached the airport, the two right lanes curved and merged, funncling the traffic to terminals 1 thru 7, domestic flights, departures. Clark didn't see the other car until it was too late. The loud sound of a crash was followed by another crash, and another.

Several car lengths ahead, Wolfee's eyes darted to the rearview mirror; Helene and Spokes turned completely around.

"I swear," Wolfee shook his head, "people don't know how to drive in L.A. The least little sprinkle—Coney Island bumper cars. They just don't understand, you gotta slow down, leave a little space between cars. See, it rains so seldom here that it never washes the oil off the road, so's all you need is a little drizzle like this and you get a pile up like that..."

Without even realizing it, Wolfee had given the tail the slip.

The rainbow van pulled up in front of the terminal. The building had an overhang which partially shielded them from the rain. It was starting to come down harder now. Wolfee continued his tirade on the appalling lack of driver savvy in L.A. Spokes and his mom took a moment to say goodbye; they stood on the sidewalk, holding onto each other's gaze.

"Willy, it's like you're a man now. You grew up so all of a

sudden." Helene wasn't going to let herself cry; she had too much eyeliner on; it would make a mess. "You know you can come home to Brooklyn anytime you want... I know you had some trouble back there... with some hoodlum..."

Right at that point in the conversation, Spokes' started to cringe.

She'd hit a nerve.

She should have sensed that something was wrong. A mother is supposed to know when her baby is hurting. He was getting very upset, and she kept on talking.

"...I know all about it... How you were hiding from some bully named Rosey. I know that's why you ran away. But you don't have to worry anymore. The word's out all over the neighborhood that he's gone, missing. No one has seen him for—"

"You don't know shit, you know that," Willy yelled at her harshly. "Rosey was a great man.... He wasn't no bully.... That's not why I ran away. I ran away because of you. So don't talk about stuff you don't know nothing about, okay."

It was quite the outburst. Even caught himself off guard. Maybe Helene was going to cry after all. She just stood there, staring at him. Wolfee was staring. The red cap who loaded the bags was staring.

When Helene finally found her voice, all she could say was "I'm sorry, Willy. I didn't mean anything. I... I..."

"Yeah, me neither.... Go on, we're getting wet standing here... You'll miss your plane."

And then, as so often happens, the heart waited till the last minute to say what it needed to say, instinctively distrusting words and preferring instead the silent press of lips; Willy gave mom a kiss on the cheek.

Wolfee tipped the red cap a ten dollar bill; at least somebody was happy.

Back inside the rainbow van—now lighter by one mom and one set of quality Gucci suitcases—was a different space, a space that had become more threatening. Wolfee plunged back onto the freeway jungle, wipers hacking away the rain—the rain which seemed determined to make Spokes cry. But he would not give the rain that satisfaction. He would not become a little boy who missed his mommy.

"So what the hell was that all about?" Wolfee snarled. "What's bothering you? Why you yelling at your mother?"

Spokes wasn't looking at Wolfee; he stared out the window. He could feel Wolfee baring his teeth, but he didn't care. He was feeling downright self-destructive: "Shut the fuck up. Mind your own business and keep your eyes on the road."

He waited, body tense, for the slap upside the head, the elbow to the ribs, something. But nothing came. They barreled past the La Tijera exit; still no punch, no slap, no word. Like the reprimand of a father that was never there. Rain pelted the roof, like metal fingers drumming their impatience. Spokes thought, *The way Wolfee's driving, I bet he's just waiting to get me home, then he's gonna let me have it.* And they were making good time; all the traffic seemed to be going the other way. The air inside the van felt heavy, like the pressure of descending underwater. Sound carries in water, and silence becomes increasingly conspicuous. Spokes would've prayed for the smack if only he could've been done with it. The guilt—like a huge scolding finger, out there, ready to descend at any time—shook at him but never struck. How he wanted to be struck.

His cheeks and his brows squeezed together and tears rolled out of his eyes. He turned to Wolfee. "I killed Rosey.... I didn't mean to... but I did... and it's your fault too. *You* gave me the angel dust. It's *your* fault too."

There, he'd said it. Between shallow gasps of breath, he managed to get it out.

Wolfee was looking straight ahead, changing lanes, starting to get over for the Sunset exit which would be coming up soon. "What are you talking about?" he wanted to know.

"You heard me," Spokes said, and it came out sounding like a challenge.

"Yeah, I heard you. And you're not making any fuckin' sense."

"It happened. I killed him. The night I saw you. In the Village. Rosey chased me back to Cockroach Art and I threw him down the elevator shaft. I don't even remember how it happened. It must've been the angel dust. When I came out of it he was dead. He never should've died that way. Me, killing the toughest guy in the projects—it shouldn't've happened."

At this point Wolfee was looking at him like he was crazy,

which was really strange coming from Wolfee.

"You know what I think, Spokes, I think you're losing it. And I don't want to hear any more of this shit. You hear me?"

Now who was acting strange! It wasn't at all like Wolfee to clam up. Spokes heard him alright—like a growl, the threatening tone reverberated in the confined space. Maybe this wasn't a good time to talk to Wolfee. Spokes decided to just sit there and not say anything for the rest of the ride.

Perhaps, not unlike a yawn or a laugh, there's a contagious element to guilt. Wolfee gnashed his teeth.

He swung the van along the tree-lined course of dips and turns that runs through the "Lifestyles of the Rich and Famous" from the 405 to the famed Sunset Strip. This was the starting point on all the Maps of the Stars. A short ways past the back entrance to UCLA, at the edge of the curb, was a sign that reminded Spokes of a monogrammed cuff; it proclaimed: Beverly Hills.

And a short ways after that, Wolfee turned onto Roxbury Drive. Spokes was eager to get back to the mansion. It was starting to feel like home. He'd head straight for the Jacuzzi. It would feel fantastic with the cool thin rain coming down. It had just about stopped. But that didn't matter—the air would still have that fresh washed feel. It would be wonderful. And afterward, he'd have Carmen whip up a little late night snack. Having money was no guarantee of happiness; but you got to choose your form of misery. Spokes was learning.

Before the rainbow van had come to a complete stop, he'd

opened the door and jumped out. He was starting to feel claustrophobic, cooped up with Mr. "Criminally Insane." Though Wolfee's getting all upset did somehow manage to make Spokes feel a little less upset. Funny how that works!

As he reached the front door with his key at the ready, Spokes heard Wolfee say, "Hey, whose car is that?"

Sure enough, there was a beat-up, mostly brown Mercury Cougar—its fenders the dull gray of primer paint. Spokes hadn't noticed it until Wolfee spotted it parked in the darkness under the bougainvillea against the side of the building. It sat there like an alley cat.

Spokes watched as Wolfee approached the car with a wariness born of territorial instinct. This was his territory, and this thing didn't belong.

There was no glass in the driver's side window. It was either rolled down all the way, or there just wasn't any. There didn't appear to be anyone in the car. Wolfee moved closer. He leaned his head toward the window. As his hand touched on the door handle, an arm—blue with tattoos and ending in the blue steel of a revolver—popped up like a jack-in-the-box. The barrel of the piece pressed against Wolfee's nose.

With the rustling of shrubs, someone stepped out and took hold of Spokes from behind. It was then that Spokes heard the looney-tune laugh. He knew instantly—it was the return of the skinheads.

~~~

Chapter 23

Where most of us end up there is no knowing, but the hellbent get where they are going.

—*James Thurber*

Under the yellowish lights by the doorway, Spokes could all too clearly see the twisted grin breathing foul against his neck. It was a face he wasn't likely to forget.

"Harry. Harry Krishna. I almost didn't recognize you without your robes." No response, just more grinning. "You look happy to see me, Har—" Spokes felt a blade come up to his throat; he shut up.

"Both me and Steve, we're real happy to see you. We been lookin' all over for you. And our van. And our money. Say, where's Tar Baby at? We were really looking forward to seeing her again."

A few feet away, Wolfee stood his ground, trying to get a good look at the guy waving the gun in his face. Staring down the barrel of a gun makes that little hole look big, like a tunnel, a tunnel with absolutely no light at the end. So Wolfee decided not to look at the gun and to concentrate instead on the gunman. He looked way too jittery to be a professional hit man. *Malfieri must be awfully pissed. He's in such a rush to zotz the Wolfee that he hires a putz like this.*

A million thoughts race around in your head when you're under the gun. It's the kind of situation about which it's often said that you never know how you're going to react. And that's true for most. But for Wolfee, who, for most of his life, had made a study of *tough*—acting tough, talking tough—it was automatic: "Gaw head. Shoot me. I dare ya, ya fuck. Chicken shit! You ain't got the balls. Asshole! You can't hurt me. You know why? I'll tell ya why! 'Cause I don't give a fuck. I ain't never been dead. So there! Gaw head. Do it. Kill me…"

What are you supposed to do when the guy you're supposed to be terrorizing is hollering at you to "Gaw head, kill me." What can you do with a guy like that? Skinhead Steve didn't know what to make of it. Here he was, pointing a gun right at the guy's face, and the guy keeps hollering at him. Not like he's scared, but like he really don't give a fuck. It was very disconcerting.

For Spokes, every second felt like borrowed time. He wasn't ready to die. The knife, just a flick of the wrist away from his voice box, scraped along his neck. Harry was getting very anxious. One false move and Spokes would never say another word again—in anybody's voice.

There had to be a way out of this. An opening.

The door to the house suddenly swung open. Carmen shouted in Spanish, "Lobito, por que estas gritando?" Which meant *Wolfee, baby, what are you yelling about?*

That was his opening. Spokes dove for the door. Carmen screamed. Two shots rang out, almost simultaneously. As he landed inside he managed to kick the door hard with the side of his leg. It slammed with a *bang*. Or maybe that was another shot. There, that was definitely a shot. And another. A bullet splintered the polished oak door, just missing Carmen, who once again screamed. Spokes quickly pulled her to the floor. They held their breaths, eyes fixed on the door.

Then came the sound. A scratching sound like someone trying to get in. They looked at each other too frightened to say a word. They listened hard. All they could hear was the scratching.

Carmen jumped up and flung open the door. Again she screamed.

Harry Krishna, knife raised, stood pressed against the air—for a moment—before he fell forward. Spokes scrambled to get out of the way as the grinning face with worried eyes came crashing down. Harry would die with that expression on his face. Several bloody holes in his back were draining the life from him.

Carmen ran recklessly out onto the driveway, carelessly stepping on Harry's body as she went.

"Wait," Spokes called after her, but it was too late. She was already out the door.

He got to his feet, a little wobbly. That's when he noticed the deep slash across his left collarbone, into his left shoulder. Blood seeping from the wound was running down his arm. He tried to press the cut closed with his right hand; blood squirted between his fingers. He could feel himself beginning to faint.

Taking several deep breaths, he looked away, to the floor, to what used to be Harry Krishna. He made sure he stepped on Harry as he stumbled outside.

The scene in the driveway was a heartbreak. Wolfee was rolling and writhing on the ground. Carmen was kneeling over him, yammering a mile a minute. Even if he understood Spanish, she was bawling like a baby, making it impossible to follow what she said. Not that it mattered. Pain needs no translation; it's the same in all languages. Wolfee was mortally wounded.

He had apparently given a good accounting of himself. Skinhead Steve's exploded cranium slumped out of the car window—shot twice in the head. The second shot was for good measure, fired from where Wolfee had fallen. Wolfee'd caught a bullet in the face and he still crawled halfway to the door of the house, firing as he went. He'd gotten them both, shot 'em dead. But it didn't seem fair; he was worth ten of them.

Spokes knelt beside his friend. In the cradle of Carmen's arms he'd stopped his thrashing, though smaller paroxysms continued to rack his body. His eyes were shaking in their sockets like two flames struggling to hold on against a strong wind.

"Spoker, my man," he grabbed Spokes' wrist; the grasp took hold of his soul, "Malfieri's the one that sent these guys."

Spokes was about to tell him different, but then, he thought better of it: *no time to explain; just listen.*

Wolfee tugged him closer. "Malfieri's the one that killed Rosey, not you. But you was half right. It was my fault. I fingered

Rosey. I had to do it, I owed the Joeys. I didn't know they was gonna kill him. Malfieri's the one pushed him. I feel bad about that. He shouldn'ta died that way."

Spokes couldn't believe what he was hearing. *Could that be? But why? Why would Malfieri kill Rosey?*

As though he read his mind, Wolfee continued, "Rosey was into the Joeys too. But Bonj was afraid to collect..." He tried to laugh but it hurt too much. "Malfieri works for Tjoepani, LaPela's uncle. He was doing LaPela a favor. Me, I was mad at Rosey 'cause a' the way he treated Freddy D and me. It was stupid, I know." His voice crackled with tears as he added, "I never meant for him to die."

Spokes pulled away. He didn't mean to. He just did. Carmen desperately tried to comfort her man, rocking him and kissing his face. She was covered in his blood.

Wolfee would not be comforted. He called to Spokes, he reached after him. "Spokes, Helene—" Mid-sentence, short rapid inhalations seized him, coming faster and faster till he could take no more air. Then it ceased.

Spokes was back, leaning over him. "What...? What about Helene?" he was shouting directly into the bloodied face.

"She didn't know..." Again the gasping for breath took control.

"She didn't know what? What...? Don't die, Wolfee. Don't die... What didn't Helene know...? Wolfee, what about my mom?"

"Junk. There's junk in the suitcases. Malfieri..." His lungs struggled to fill again, like stabbing hiccups.

He was gone.

He always knew he'd meet a violent death.

Spokes looked around, at the driveway of dead men, and then up into the dark misty blue. He couldn't help thinking that Wolfee, the "criminally insane" tough guy from East New York, would not be disappointed.

~~~

Chapter 24

Blood follows blood.

—De Foe

Three murders—it wouldn't take long before the place was crawling with cops. And Spokes literally rolled out the red carpet for those who would come to investigate: a trail of blood followed his frantic path through the house. He ran to his room to get some money; droplets of red fell everywhere, splattering the dresser draws inside and out. There was another pool of the red stuff at the foot of the sliding closet doors in Wolfee's room.

It was there Spokes found the original suitcases that Helene had brought with her from Mexico; inside each, a false bottom. That was all Spokes needed to see. It confirmed Wolfee's story. It justified his own mounting sense of urgency.

The crimson trail finally ended in one of the downstairs bathrooms where he hastily wrapped an entire roll of gauze around his shoulder.

Acting on instinct, Spokes knew he had to get away from there as fast as he could. There was no time to lose.

He took the skinhead's car. He wasn't sure why he decided

to take that car instead of the van, he just knew it was the right way to go. Maybe 'cause it was less conspicuous. He also decided not to take the freeway. He would take Santa Monica Boulevard to Sepulveda, then Sepulveda all the way.

It took all his effort, but he was doing it, moving slowly and staying in the right-hand lane. But there was nothing he could do about his mind: it was racing wildly in all directions. He glanced at the dash—the fuel gauge showed more than half full. *As long as this hunk-a'-junk doesn't break down... One step at a time*, he told himself. The steering wheel was a little shaky and it pulled to the left. This car had obviously been in a wreck. Which was pretty much how Spokes felt. He'd been reduced to the use of only his right arm.

A red light. He was glad for the brief rest. He pressed his left arm between his body and the door trying to still the throbbing.

The light changed and he lurched forward. He barely managed to take control of the wheel in time to avoid hitting an oncoming truck. To be more precise, a battered panel truck with the Pacific Bell logo on the side.

"Look out!" Olsen yelled from the passenger seat.

Olsen and Clark just missed Spokes—in more ways than one.

"That was a close call."

Responding to Olsen, Clark said, "Look out? Me? Look out? I wasn't the one veering into oncoming traffic!"

"I didn't mean to imply that you were," Olsen was quick to explain. "That guy must have been drunk. I just meant for you to look out for him. One accident per day is all I can handle."

"So what you mean to say is that you think the accident at the airport was my fault?"

"I don't mean to say anything, okay. Never mind. It's been a long day..."

Clark let it drop, focusing his attention on the road ahead: "The way this vehicle's handling, we'll be lucky if we make it to Roxbury Drive. It's no longer roadworthy. It really shouldn't be driven—that's why I didn't take the freeway—but we have no choice, we can't let them get away." He gripped the wheel tighter and steered with determination along the eastbound boulevard, while Spokes continued on his way—westbound, to the airport.

Spokes got a seat on a midnight flight out of LAX.

The in-flight movie turned out to be one he'd already seen, so he closed his eyes and tried to rest. There was no way he was going to be able to sleep. Still, he spent almost the entire flight with his eyes closed.

And as he sat at thirty thousand feet, ticking off the minutes, he found that he was not alone inside his head. Voices crowded in: Wolfee, Rosey, even Sayer. They were all there with him, real as can be. Like an advisory council, they prepared him for what he must do. What was needed was not so much a plan—there were too many variables—but rather a frame of mind. If he was going to follow through, he was going to have to maintain the momentum.

Riding the jet stream, the 747 landed him at JFK at eight

o'clock the following morning.

~~~

Chapter 25

A woman's hopes are woven of sunbeams; a shadow annihilates them.

—*George Eliot*

The dynamics of the relationship between Helene Freeman and Jimmy Malfieri was something neither one of them could understand. It was something that came over them, like when two people share a cold, the kind of cold that you just can't seem to shake; it has to run its course.

Helene had arrived back in New York wearing reddish framed sunglasses that were too big for her face, with lenses to provide the proverbial rose-colored view of the world. She knew that things hadn't been right with her and Jimmy, but she told herself the excuses that women tell themselves: *it all happened so fast, he doesn't know yet how much he loves me; I can make it work.* It had been so long since she was involved with a man, she'd forgotten what it was all about. Maybe she never really knew. Times had changed. Helene Freeman had changed. Maybe she was expecting too much.

The fact that Jimmy had taken such an interest in helping her arrange this business trip was, she thought, a positive sign. It showed that he was willing to be supportive and at the same time accept her as a capable, independent person. Considering his background, that was quite an accomplishment. Whatever the problem was—she was sure it was a thing of the past. Somehow, this trip and seeing Willy had convinced her that everything was going to be alright. Knowing that Willy was safe, knowing where he was and that she could pick up the phone and talk to him, that he was still her son and that he still loved her—that made all the difference in the world. It cleared away the distraction that had hovered over her 24/7 ever since she first began seeing Jimmy. She felt sure that that was the cloud over their relationship. From here on, nothing but clear skies.

From the terminal at JFK she went directly to Lot 8, where she had parked her car one week ago. Jimmy had suggested she do it that way, which was smart. It ended up costing no more than the taxi fare and it was a lot more convenient.

It was also smart of him for another reason: he had people at the parking lot on his payroll. He knew the moment she retrieved her car.

The moment she passed under the upraised arm of the barrier gate, a parking lot attendant hopped onto his motorcycle and tagged along behind. He made no attempt to hide, yet went unnoticed by Helene. His instructions didn't say anything about being discreet: he was to make sure that she wasn't being followed; to make sure she got where she was going.

She drifted out into the sparse pre-dawn traffic skirting the borough. From where she sat the city looked like Christmas morning: shiny presents wrapped in twinkling ribbon. From a distance bright lights have a way of hiding defects, of glossing over the rot in foundations, the filth in the corners. And then, when you get right down into it, sometimes, the rot and the filth is all you can see.

There were no parking spaces along Glenwood Road so Helene ended up finding a spot way up Ralph Avenue where there were no sidewalks, only the lots.

Stepping from her car—the image of the streets of Beverly Hills still clear in her mind—what a difference a day makes! She looked at the neighborhood like it was a strange, evil place. Before, she'd never noticed all the litter: It pressed against a sewer grate in a giant drift of newspaper, cellophane wrappers, cigarette butts, bottles and cans; the entire avenue was lined with refuse—like a garbage can turned upside down.

Holding her new Rodeo Drive luggage close, she began walking quickly down the avenue. Her heels resounded on the asphalt, seeming to flutter like palpitations. The jingling of her bracelets bounced out like ripples from a shiny lure.

Something made her stop—and listen.

The streets were empty; not a breeze was moving. All she could hear was the static hum of streetlamps. She pressed her wrists to her sides to try and still her passage through the night— and not wake whatever might be lurking in the shadows.

A car engine shifted gears off the distance, straining against the night.

It began to occur to Helene that, as usual, she hadn't

thought things out: this wasn't at all smart, arriving so late at night. She should've called Jimmy from the airport; he could've come to meet her. This was not the same stubborn, fiercely independent Helene of just a few months earlier. Having a man in her life, a man to protect her, had allowed her to let down her guard, to own her fears and her vulnerability.

By now she was practically running through the still night air. She reached the entrance of the building: a small solitary figure racing to safety.

There was no lock on the outside door; the hallway offered no reassurance, only government-green walls illuminated by a stark bulb under wire mesh. Wire mesh was a theme that ran throughout the project decor: chicken wire sandwiched in the glass of the hallway doors, in the little window on the elevator door.

She jiggled the elevator button impatiently.

She glanced at her mailbox—force of habit—fifth from the right, bottom row. Empty... *Jimmy must have brought it up.* He had a key to the place; she had asked him to look in while she was away: check the mail, feed the goldfish. She half expected him to forget.

The light bulb on the undercarriage of the elevator shone in the little window as it made its slow descent. Helene nervously pulled at the handle on the door, though she knew she had to wait; the door wouldn't open until the inner mechanical door had completely withdrawn.

About to step in, Helene remembered the safety mirror in

the upper corner. The mirrors had been installed throughout the projects after several incidents. Muggers would wait, concealed in a corner of the elevator, and then when the victim got on...

Helene paused to check the mirror—the coast was clear. She stepped inside.

In a minute she would be on the fifth floor, safe in her own apartment behind a dead bolt lock. It just wasn't a safe place to live anymore. Maybe it never was. But when you're a young mother first starting out and you don't have much choice, you tend not to notice.

As she fit her key into the top lock, she was surprised to find the door unlocked. She pushed lightly and the door opened a crack. She peered in—and when she saw Jimmy sitting at the dinette table, she burst in and ran straight into his arms.

"What a wonderful surprise!—finding you here."

Not until she was trapped in his embrace did she look in his eyes.

She had less to fear outside on the street.

~~~

Chapter 26

There's Ransom in a Voice

—Emily Dickinson

Spokes observed: there were too many colors in the sky over New York; that many colors belong in a sunset, not an early morning.

From a phone booth at the airport he dialed his mother's number.

It picked up on the second ring; Jimmy Malfieri said, "Hello... Hello... Who is this?"

He was answered by a familiar voice, a harsh whisper grating through the receiver: "Malfieri, my man..."

It was Wolfee.

"I been expecting your call.... So, Wolfee, you in New York? ...Now what? You got some kinda plan how you're gonna work this nasty little piece a' business...? I gotta tell ya, you're making a big mistake. Nobody rips me off. It just ain't done."

He heard Wolfee, bold as can be, tell him, "Save the tough talk, Jimmy."

In the background, Spokes could hear crying. It was Helene.

223

Spokes bit his lip. He moved his wounded left shoulder so as to start a burning pain coursing through his body. He needed to feel the physical to steel him against the emotional: some kind of subconscious override. And when he swallowed the pain, he was able to continue.

All Malfieri heard was the confident and contemptuous voice of a motherfucker who couldn't've cared less about a mother's tears.

"You ain't man enough to stand face to face, you gotta sneak up behind and push 'em when they ain't looking—like you did Rosey!"

"Wolfee, you got a big mouth—and I'm the one who's gonna shut it for you."

"You! Don't make me laugh. You're one a' them macho guys likes to pick on tiny women. I think you better stick to beating up girls. That's about your speed.

"And Jimmy... just so you know, I had your scam figured out the moment Helene mentioned your name. She didn't have anything to do with pulling the switcheroo on you, Jimbo—I did that all by myself. Poor Helene didn't even know what was in them suitcases. But you already know that."

"You're gonna be sorry you didn't mind your own fucking business, Wolfee. Take my advice: hand over what's mine and then run, and keep running. Maybe, just maybe, you'll get to live."

"Will you stop with these threats already. How many times I gotta tell you, you ain't that tough. Now stop beatin' your gums and just listen... Go to work as usual. I'll call you later at the Regent with the time and place. In the meanwhile, put together twenty-five big ones." Spokes had simply picked a nice round number. The real Wolfee wouldn't've done it any different. It wasn't like he thought for a minute that Malfieri would go along with it. "Now that shouldn't be a problem for a wise guy like you. See what a reasonable guy I can be! You're getting a bargain."

As Malfieri listened he rubbed his fingers lightly against the sure-grip handle of his Beretta—a fine Italian weapon.

When Spokes finally put down the phone he felt a wave of fatigue sweep over him, threatening to stop him cold. He couldn't let that happen. Again he shook his left arm and the pain bit into his shoulder. Like a shot of straight caffeine it picked him right up and kept him going. He was learning a lot about pain that he hadn't known before.

He hailed a cab and headed for the old neighborhood.

Standing on the Canarsie side of Ralph Avenue, looking across to the projects, it was like he was seeing the place for the first time. He took a step back. It was, of course, familiar, but at the same time he'd never seen it from this vantage point. It all looked so much smaller. What used to be the center of his world was just an ordinary city block. The buildings were only six stories high. The streets seemed narrower than he remembered. Even the weeping willow at the mouth of the lots seemed smaller.

He looked across to the fifth floor window, to the apartment that had been his home. There were curtains on the living room window. Helene had hung them with great pride. To her, they were something of status symbol. Most of the other windows in the projects had only shades.

He stood there waiting for the curtains to move. How many times before had he stood there? When he was very young he would stand in the grass directly below the window and holler up: "Helene... Helene..." One time, some of the blue-uniformed maintenance men asked him if Helene was a nanny hired to watch him while his mother went to work. They thought it odd that he called his mother *Helene,* rather than *Mom,* or maybe it was because Helene, herself, looked to be no more than a girl. Whatever, *Helene* was what he called her. It was easier that way. There were so many kids in the projects; whenever some kid would holler up "Mom," half a dozen windows would open.

As he grew older and began to wander further from the watchful eye of the fifth floor window, it would be Helene who would stand at the window to call out, to remind him to bring back a quart of milk or a loaf of bread. To remind him to stay out of the lots.

The crack of a BB gun interrupted his thoughts. It was coming from the lots, behind him. Hesitant to take his eyes off the window, he tore himself away, slowly making his way for the cover of that mangy undergrowth.

Once inside he followed the sound along the path through the weeds. Shortly he came upon none other than Jeffrey

Munchik. He was standing on a mound of dirt at the edge of the clearing. He was with two other kids: Robby Van Wert and Mitch Telvee's little brother, Michael. Munch was a full foot taller and broader across than either one of them. Two dirt bikes lay on the ground a few feet away. They were taking turns firing a Daisy air rifle. On the other side of the mound, about ten yards away, an old milk truck was overturned in a ditch. It was the crowning glory on a rotting pile of junk. When one of the boys would throw a rock at it, rats would come running out. And they would shoot at the rats.

Spokes crossed the clearing, heading toward the hunting party.

Just as he came on the scene, a big daddy rat came charging out from under a stack of rusted-out hubcaps. Then, instead of scurrying for refuge in the junk heap, like the other rats, he stood brazenly out in the open. His home sweet home had been disturbed and he wanted to see who dared threaten his domain.

Munch fired and hit.

The rat flipped in the air and came down on his side, feet flailing. He fired twice more and the feet stopped.

"Think he's dead?" Robby asked.

"He's still alive!" exclaimed Michael, pointing excitedly. "I just saw his head move."

Munch picked up a big rock and went down into the ditch, where he crushed its head. "Not anymore..."

With the hunt successfully concluded, Munch acknowledged Spokes with a nod, then a smile. He was glad to have one more witness to his moment of triumph.

Spokes didn't consider Robby and Michael his friends—they were too young, just kids—but they knew who he was. And it wasn't his exploits as the Fifteen Year Old Mystic that earned him notoriety. It was his reputation as freestylin' bike rider extraordinaire that carried weight with these boys.

As Munch climbed up out of the ditch he held out a mitt for Spokes to give him a hand up. Spokes obliged. Grasping Munchik's left hand awkwardly in his right hand and leaning backwards, he pulled. As Munch crested the ridge, there was a good-natured laugh, followed by words "Your mother." His right arm swung wide. Then a solid sock landed on Spokes' left shoulder.

Spokes stood there for a moment, the word "Nooo!" stuck on his face. His eyes were swimming like a cartoon character who just got whomped on the head; then he collapsed—out cold.

He came to a minute later and found himself stretched out inside the latest in the long line of clubhouses. The boys had done a fine job on this one. They must've raided a construction site. Fresh lumber framed most of the boxcar style structure except for one wall where they ran out of wood and substituted part of a billboard. The room was about twelve feet long and six feet across; the ceiling was not quite high enough for Munchik to stand, but almost. The floor was dug out to allow for a low profile; from outside, surrounding weeds were high enough to provide concealment.

Like clubhouses everywhere, an essential element of its appeal came from it being clandestine. Within its walls kids told stories, shared secrets, and sworn loyalties—all made special by hallowed ground. And of all the clubhouses the lots had ever been home to, of all the stories told, secrets shared, and loyalties sworn—to this clubhouse, on this morning, Spokes brought with him the best ever.

~~~

Chapter 27

If you got 'em by the balls, their hearts and minds will follow.

—*Anonymous*

Spokes was absorbed by sleep like a puddle into a giant sponge.

He wasn't missing much. Throughout the projects the afternoon wore on with a vagueness—indistinct, like a dream hours after waking. It seemed to stretch on and on, longer than an afternoon is supposed to.

But for Michael Telvee, it had become a day with a mission—a mission that had run into a bit of a snag. Michael didn't usually hang around the big playground. His older brother, Mitch, was sixteen; he hung out there—all the time. In a manner of speaking, it was Mitch Telvee's office: he sold dime bags on the corner by the pizza place. Mitch didn't like having his kid brother "spying" on him while he was working. For some peculiar reason, on this particular afternoon, Michael Telvee had taken it upon himself to hang around on that corner—*his brother's corner.* Mitch told him to get lost—about ten times. The kid just wouldn't take a hint. As the afternoon waned the corner got busier. More of Mitch's buddies began to congregate at the pizza place. Mitch felt increasingly embarrassed at having his little brother inflicted upon him. So, predictably, what ended up happening was that their touching little display of brotherly love became the main event of the afternoon, holding center stage on the corner by Fat George's Pizza Place.

You'd have to be blind not to see that these two were brothers: the same long torsos astride short slightly bowed legs, doughy complexions, wavy red hair. Mitch was just a larger version, was all. They both had reputations as scrappers and it was generally held that neither fought anyone else as fiercely as they fought each other.

Mitch stood intransigently between Michael and the door to the pizza place. "Now get the fuck outta here… and I mean it!"

Mitch sounded like he meant it.

"I wanna get an Italian ice!" Michael sniveled; he was on the verge of tears. He rubbed the back of his hand across his face, leaving the dirt to streak his cheeks like war paint.

"Look at yourself, you little snot nose—"

Michael, his head down, rushed straight at him.

These two were old hands at sibling rivalry; it would take more of a fake than that to pull off a successful surprise attack. Mitch easily sidestepped the charge, spinning his brother around and throwing him to the ground. Hard.

And if that wasn't painful and humiliating enough, Mitch took Michael's bike and threw it into the street. Laughing at his stupid little brother, he turned and walked back to his buddies.

That did it! Michael rushed him again; this time with murder in his eyes. He delivered a head butt to the kidneys and locked his arms around Mitch's waist in a mighty effort to tackle the bigger Telvee.

He wouldn't go down.

Little Telvee did manage to push Big Telvee up against the wall of the pizza place, slamming him there and literally holding him off the ground, while Big Telvee bombarded savage blows down on his little brother's shoulders.

Once again, Michael was getting the worst of it.

It was frightening to see such violence between brothers. Those gathered on the corner knew better than to break it up. A couple of clowns on the sidelines started to sing: "He ain't heavy, he's my brother."

Then, like a shot fired into the air, a shrill howl was raised above the ruckus, bringing the goings-on up sharp.

The sound had come from Mitch. His back was as straight as a rod. His eyes were opened almost as wide as his mouth. He wasn't moving, not an iota. Michael had gotten a firm grip on the situation.

"You move an inch and I'll tear 'em out by the roots. I mean it!"

It sounded like he meant it.

At this rather delicate juncture, who should arrive but none other than the party for whom the younger Telvee was secretly lying in wait: the big-finned black Caddy came from the alley behind the building and muscled its way up onto the sidewalk, creating its own parking space a few feet short of where the Telvee brothers stood frozen like the work of some whimsical sculptor.

The way Bonj extracted his bulk from the Cadillac gave the impression he was getting out of a sports car. Ever since Rosey disappeared Bonj seemed to have more weight to throw around. He and LaPela were now the undisputed badasses on the block. From within their fleshy sockets the beady eyes surveyed the statue. Bonj scoffed his disapproval: "I don't wanna have no roughhousing out here. Me and Joey wanna have a nice," and here he emphasized the word, "...*quiet* dinner." He waved his hand like it was a scepter. "You wanna fuck around, go across the street to the park. That's what parks are for."

Fat George, standing in the doorway, had been watching the fight. He shouted a greeting to Bonj and LaPela in Italian, to which Bonj shouted back, also in Italian—*two orders of linguini with clams and red sauce*. It wasn't on the menu, it was a special dish that George made up special for Bonj.

As the two Joeys prepared to follow George back to their table, Bonj, again turning his attention to the rabble, added, "I ain't gonna tell yas so nice the next time. Am I making myself clear?"

A rhetorical question. And of course no one answered. Silence implied assent. Anything else was asking for trouble.

The moment Bonj disappeared inside, Mitch dropped to the sidewalk, holding his balls, biting his lower lip in pain.

Brother Michael made a mad dash for his bike and peeled

out of there fast as he could.

On the other side of the projects, across from the lots, in front of 1736, Robby Van Wert was passing the time freestyling: standing with one foot on the pedal, one foot alongside the rear sprocket, he balanced on the back tire, bouncing and turning like on a unicycle.

It was a busy corner, with two bus stops, one on either side; four different lines made stops there. So even though, according to project parlance, Robby didn't belong there, no one noticed that the kid had been hanging around all day long.

The kid was really a lookout, and he had just spotted the person he was on the lookout for.

It was almost five o'clock when Jimmy Malfieri came down the steps of the building, moving on a quick but cautious stride. He had on a particularly bold pin-striped suit, the kind the old-fashioned gangsters wore—the style was coming back. His eyes scanned the foreground, going right past the kid on the bicycle. On the return sweep—still nothing out of the ordinary. The sight of a kid pedaling across Ralph Avenue toward the lots wasn't something to draw his attention.

Robby disappeared past the gateway of the weeping willow. He made wild Indian sounds with his tongue like a scout sounding the alarm: it was time for Spokes to get up.

Jimmy Malfieri was going to work at the Regent Supper Club. Spokes was *going to work* on Malfieri. By now, Jimmy's thoughts were distracted, wanting to crush that mongrel dog,

Wolfee. He expected he might get his chance before the night was out. He didn't expect it to come so soon. Upon arriving at the club he was told that there was a call waiting: "Mr. Malfieri, a Mr. Wolfee on the line. Says you know what it's about."

Caught momentarily off guard, Malfieri answered as though he were talking to himself: "It's okay... I'll take it in my office." He went to the end of the corridor, to the door marked PRIVATE. Closing the door behind him, he stared at the phone on his desk, at the blinking button.

He picked up the phone, pushed in the button: "This is Malfieri."

Instantly Wolfee told him, "The carriage storage room in back of 1736 in one hour. Alone."

Malfieri started to say something—but was abruptly cut off.

Spokes slammed down the receiver. He tilted his head back as if that might keep the tears from falling.

He was sitting in his mother's bedroom. He was holding back his anger and sadness. It was his own unaltered adolescent voice that screamed inside his head: *Why Helene? My poor little mother! She didn't do anything. She doesn't deserve this.*

Helene was semiconscious, just barely holding on. Malfieri had beaten her pretty badly.

Michael and Robby were getting ready to take her down to the car. Munchik had gotten his driver's license—God help us all!—and he was going to take her to Kings County Hospital.

Spokes had other business to attend to. Now more than ever. He took a deep breath, cleared his throat, and picked up the

235

phone.

On the third ring it was answered by George: "George's I-talian Restaurant."

"Listen, George, this is Wolfee. Is—"

"Wolfee, long-a time you no come around. How you been...?"

There was a clatter of falling silverware, the sound of a chair scraping against the floor as it was being pushed back from the table. Bonj moved surprisingly fast for someone his size. He yanked the phone out of Fat George's hand.

"Wolfee, you're a dead man, you hear me? A dead man!"

"Bonj, my man, my buddy, calm down or you gonna give yourself indigestion." Wolfee sounded so cool. He would've dug on hearing himself talk to Bonj this way. "I got the money I owe you... but you're gonna have to come get it." Spokes smiled at the silence on the other end; Bonj didn't know what to say. Wolfee was calling the shots. "That's right. You heard right. I got your money. And I think maybe I'm gonna shove it up your ass."

~~~

Chapter 28

When in doubt, have two guys come through the door with guns.

—Raymond Chandler

If the projects were a living breathing thing, in back of Spokes' building would be the belly.

A long driveway ran the length of the building. Several times a month, a tanker truck would snake its way down the oily incline to hook a hose into the ground. It sat there for hours while it pumped heating fuel into the beast.

At the end of the driveway there was a long ramp leading down into the basement of the building. In the basement was the boiler room, and a storage room for bicycles and carriages.

Spokes started down that long driveway. He had Michael Telvee's Daisy air rifle at his side pointing to the oily tar-covered surface at his feet. Orange and pink clouds streaked on high. To his right, his shadow marched across the grass and stretched ten feet tall against the building wall. To his left was a single-story garage which housed maintenance equipment: riding lawn mowers, a couple old orange dump trucks, and snowplow blades used to clear the walkways. The four wide garage doors were closed now. By five o'clock—no, by four thirty—all the maintenance men had gone home.

The incline made it feel not so much like walking as like being drawn.

Ahead loomed the smoke stack. All the buildings in the projects had incinerators; every roof had a chimney, but only behind 1736 was there a smoke stack. It was a rite of passage for boys growing up in the projects to throw a ball onto the roof. And once he could do that he'd try to throw a ball completely over a building. But only a very few would ever be able to throw a ball into the smoke stack. From high above the rooftops it watched over the projects, its lightning rod antenna waiting on the sky. Spokes stopped in his tracks and take a moment to look up. Rosey had been able to throw a ball into the smoke stack.

He marched on—down the driveway.

It was on that driveway that he learned to ride. All in an afternoon. Several neighbors remarked: that Willy Freeman is one persistent little kid. On a bicycle too big for the five year old, without anyone to run behind, he'd kept at it. By the end of the day he could ride a two wheeler.

Spokes was at the end of the driveway.

He followed the handrail down the ramp to the basement door.

When he was a kid it used to scare him to go down there. He and the other little kids used to go running into the basement, scream and yell, and then come running out again as fast as they could. Sometimes one of the maintenance men—a good-natured lot—would play their silly little game. A big black blue-uniformed maintenance man would see them in the hall and put his hands up like a bear and send them laughing and running into the daylight—having just escaped the bogeyman.

On the other side of the basement door was a labyrinth of hallways. Spokes' childhood games had taught him at least three other ways out of the convolutions of underground passageways. The air was cool and stale; it always seemed ten degrees colder down there, where the rough concrete walls were cold and damp to the touch. The air was filled with the constant drone of the boiler room, like the stomach of a giant—grumbling and pinging. A dank, dark subterranean viscera.

There were two doors on the right, a good thirty feet apart; they both led into the same room—the carriage room. Spokes went to the far door, opened it, and flipped the light switch. The lights didn't go on right away, but flickered first and then held, white and harsh, illuminating an enormous storage space filled with baby carriages, junk bicycles, and old steamer trunks stacked in corners. Support columns, each formed of a thick block of concrete set at regular intervals, divided the space. The ceiling was a network of pipes. Along a side wall several wire mesh lockers provided storage for odd pieces of furniture. The whole place was steeped in the smell of rust and mildew, and other people's things.

Spokes still had time. He could still get his ass the hell out of there.

Malfieri arrived ahead of schedule, whistling warily as he approached the unfamiliar surroundings. No actual sound passed his lips, only air. And even that ceased as he descended the ramp to the basement. Proceeding slowly, he stopped outside the carriage room door and drew his gun.

He threw open the door.

He peered into the darkness, making no move to enter.

He waded in, putting each foot down as if the floor might be pulled out from under him at any moment. His eyes jumped from pillar to post. He felt for the light switch; it was where he expected—next to the door. He flicked it on. Nothing happened. Thinking it was broken, he flipped it on and off several times. Finally, the room flickered like an old movie projector. It was *show time*. The lights came on. Malfieri's head bobbed as it rotated, sending his gaze up and down the rows of bicycles. Both arms extended, taking a two-handed grip on his gun, his feet snatched up jerky steps. It was as though with each step he was expecting to say—*gotcha!*

In that fashion he had made it halfway across the room. Then he heard something—a footfall on the ramp outside. He wheeled around and leapt for the light switch. He hit the lights, then pulled the door closed—careful to not let it slam.

There were two clicks, almost simultaneous—the carriage room door clicked closed, the outside basement door clicked open.

Pressed up against the concrete pillar closest to the second door, Malfieri waited. His gun waited. He held it with both hands between his legs, like he was holding his dick.

Submerged in the pitch black stillness, his ears picked up on the barely audible sound in the corridor just beyond the first door—the click of a round being chambered.

The door swung inward. A bulky shadow blocked the pale light from the hallway. The shadow reached in and began to feel around for the light switch.

Malfieri was careful not to make a sound. He wasn't about to give his position away.

A hand found the switch. The overhead lights began to flicker; the whole room appeared to blink.

That's when confusion rained down on Jimmy Malfieri—in a flash.

There was a rustling noise behind him.

Wolfee's voice was right there behind him: "You mess wit da Wolfee, you messin' wit one bad motherfucker."

A flimsy shot, like the crack of a BB gun, echoed sharply off the walls.

Malfieri felt a sting on his leg; he jumped back away from the pillar and a real blast reverberated. It came from the bulky shadow by the door. The bullet caught Jimmy in the chest and spun him around. He fired his Beretta three times as he sunk to the ground. Two of the shots found the ample target provided by the figure in the doorway and sent the shadow sailing back out the way he came.

It all went down in a few flickering seconds.

And as the flicker took hold, the aftermath came to light.

Spokes crawled out from his hiding place behind an old steamer trunk to look around. His ears were ringing. He stood up to a faint smell of gunpowder in the air. He inhaled deeply as he looked down at Malfieri lying face up on the cold concrete floor. Holding a scolding finger over the dying hoodlum, Spokes offered an inane warning: "I don't ever want you going near my mother again."

Malfieri responded by gurgling blood.

Suddenly there were footsteps racing through the hallway.

The thought raced through Spokes' mind: *If it's the cavalry, they're too late.*

A half dozen men wearing blue *FBI* windbreakers swarmed into the carriage room. Leading the charge—Clark and Olsen. Guns drawn, they bore down on Spokes.

"Drop it!" Clark ordered.

The Daisy air rifle clattered to the ground.

~~~

Chapter 29

With words we govern men.

—Disraeli

Mourners bring flowers. Visitors to the Baron Hirsch Cemetery on Staten Island leave pebbles on the headstones to mark their visits; that was where Spokes first observed the custom—on a visit to the grave of his father.

Spokes picked a smooth round pebble and placed it on the ledge of the cornerstone of the new luxury apartments. He was standing around the corner from Bleecker Street, at the site of what used to be Cockroach Art. There's probably no place on earth more conducive to reflection than beside a grave. This particular grave just happened to be a thirty-four story building. The old factory building had been demolished using explosives, crumbling neatly down as if all along it had been only so much ash and dust.

The body in the subbasement was never discovered—or if it was, the job foreman didn't want to get behind schedule.

What the hell!—it did make one monumental fuckin' tombstone! That's for sure!

Spokes couldn't stand there much longer. There was a biting wind on the loose. The kind of wind that's a precursor to snow. It pushed its way down the concrete corridors, harassing anyone and everyone on the street.

Spokes pulled the fur collar of his coat up about his face and turned to start across the street when a voice called to him: "Willy. Willy Freeman."

He spun around.

He knew the voice, but he didn't recognize the rest. Not at first.

"Chance?" he asked, his head jutting out to get a better look at the person coming toward him. "Chance Langston?"

The man standing before him looked older than his friend Chance. This man had a beard, a dirty matted beard. He was puffy with layer upon layer of raggedy clothes. Many different pant legs stuck out at the bottom of his trousers. He had to be wearing his entire wardrobe.

Chance assured him, "It really is me!" Taking Spokes' hand, he shook it until the glimmer of recognition finally lit on Spokes' face.

They hugged each other.

There was a minute of standing there awkwardly; and then, as the wind kicked up, "Hey, I know..." Spokes offered, "How about a pizza...? Whadaya say?"

Chance didn't say anything. He just looped his arm over Spokes' shoulder and steered him in the direction of the Pizza Box.

They had a lot to catch up on.

They ordered a large pie with garlic and anchovies, and a couple cans of soda.

There was so much to tell, Spokes hardly knew where to start. The last time he saw Chance, he and Pat were boarding a Greyhound. That seemed the logical place to begin. But first, there was something he had to know.

He asked Chance: Had he seen Pat? Was she alright?

Willy was pleased by what he heard. Pat had a job singing backup in a gospel group, on the road much of the time. She was doing well. From what Chance said, she had even been able to help her mother and brother—the family could finally move to a better neighborhood, somewhere in Queens.

Spokes sat back in his chair.

The pizza came and Chance began devouring it. Spokes wasn't very hungry.

What he did need—more than anything—was a friend to talk to. Someone who would understand. *Chance Langston. What better person!* Here was the man who'd first encouraged Spokes to develop his talent.

It was that talent that had both saved and enslaved.

He told the whole incredible story: How he and Pat were kidnapped by skinheads disguised as Hare Krishna's and barely escaped with their lives—and the skinhead's van containing ten thousand dollars; of how he was received as the Fifteen Year Old Mystic whose coming marked the start of the New Age; and how he went to live in a mansion in Beverly Hills, and there was

Carmen the maid and Wolfee, his own personal bodyguard. They sat there for an hour as Spokes recounted the events that went into making the proverbial bed in which he now slept. There was the part about his mom, how she was unwittingly used by Malfieri.

When Spokes came to the part about Wolfee's heroic finish, Chance, who'd been following the story with confoundingly little expression, became animated, banging the table several times with the palm of his hand and biting his lower lip. Spokes ignored the outburst. He didn't think anything of it—Chance, just being his usual weird self.

And just as quickly as his attention had piqued, so it was that he settled back down to the pizza at hand. He shook a flurry of hot peppers onto his next slice.

Spokes went on with his story. He explained that they didn't know it at the time, but the FBI had been keeping an eye on the Regent Supper Club—even before Helene started going with Malfieri. They had a long-standing interest in the owner, Don Tjoepani.

Helene, thank God, was out of the woods, doing well, making a full recovery.

It was Helene who led the Feds to Spokes. They were on her trail the moment she arrived in Los Angeles. A Beverly Hills mansion, the Atlantis Fellowship, a fifteen year old channeler—those FBI guys didn't know what to make of it.

Later, back in Brooklyn, they had Helene's phone tapped, and they found themselves eavesdropping on a conversation between the then-dead Wolfee and the now-dead Malfieri.

They began to see the practical applications of Spokes' talent.

To that end there came a mixed blessing. When the shit hit the fan, they cleaned up the mess in the carriage room, not to mention the even bigger mess outside the carriage room—Joey "Bonj" Bonjonela died on his way to the hospital. It took three ambulance attendants and a begrudging FBI agent to lift him onto the gurney. Malfieri's bullet had ruptured a major artery; he bled into his gut.

A garden hose could wash the blood off the concrete. Coming up with a story that would wash—now that was something else altogether.

Malfieri represented months of surveillance—shot to hell. They had to have something to show for it.

Why not Spokes!

They told the press that one Stanley "Wolfee" Wolfe of East New York was responsible not only for the carnage at 1024 North Roxbury Drive in Beverly Hills, California, but also for the shoot-out behind 1736 Ralph Avenue in Brooklyn, New York. Very tidy, very slick. Once they flew Wolfee's body back to New York, nobody would be the wiser. All the evidence was there to corroborate the story.

And Wolfee had earned his place in the annals of crime after all. *He was one bad motherfucker!* He would have been proud.

The newspapers had a field day. Harry Krishna and Skinhead Steve turned out to be members of an outlaw white supremacist group—no surprise there!—wanted in three states in connection with armed robberies. And of course, the obituaries on Malfieri and Bonjonela were somewhat short of sterling—two alleged mob enforcers. As might be expected, Wolfee gleaned his share of favorable press—he was practically a candidate for the Congressional Medal of Honor.

The Fifteen Year Old Mystic dropped out of sight, never to be heard from again. The word out of California was that this world wasn't yet ready for him; he was called back to the Beyond. His disappearance wasn't what you'd call front page news. It was the kind of item that was only of interest to a small circle of flakes. There was even one Southern California channeler who claimed to be in contact with the spirit, guide and teacher of *Spokes*.

The more earthbound Spokes, however, was on ice for the time being. Technically, he was part of the witness relocation program. The FBI didn't want him talking to anyone. He wasn't even supposed to be out. After all, he was their secret weapon. They had him ferreted away in a "safe house"—it felt more like prison—where they had him listen endlessly to wiretap recordings of various crime-figures: Columbian drug lords, Mafia Dons, even some white-collar criminals. They had big plans for Willy. In the world of crime, business is conducted by verbal agreement. A talent such as his could come in very handy.

Willy had come to the end of his story.

He looked across at Chance, who was nodding empathetically. Spokes suddenly got the awful feeling that

Chance was about to say something like ...*Don't you just hate it when that happens*. But he didn't say anything. He just continued to nod and smile. Smile and nod.

Then it occurred to Spokes, here he was talking and talking, only about himself. It was obvious that Chance had been through a hell of a lot since they last saw each other.

He asked, "So, Chance, now is your turn. Tell me, what's been happening with you...? How's the act coming along...? Do you still see...?" Spokes couldn't think of her name. "What's-her-name...? Lucrecia."

Before Spokes could even get the name out, Chance began to shake his head, short flinching movements dodging invisible slaps. "What's... been... happening... with... me," he repeated. The way he said it, it was as if he were trying out a foreign language.

A thought crossed Spokes' mind.

No, he told himself, pushing off any such notion.

He asked Chance again, more slowly this time: "Yeah, what's happening with you?"

And this time Chance responded. Somewhere inside a circuit was completed. His eyes lit. He'd thought of something important to tell his old friend: "I met Andy Kaufman. We're going to start an act together—the Comedy Team of Kaufman and Langston."

He was serious.

"Chance, Andy Kaufman...? Andy Kaufman's dead. Remember...? He died real young... of a heart attack."

"No, that's what they want us to think."

"Who? Chance. That's what *who* wants us to think?"

"The government. The government wants us to think that."

"But why? Chance...? Why would the government want us to think that Andy Kaufman was dead?"

There was no stumping him. He had an answer for that one. *Boy, did he have an answer!* Giving Spokes a look as if to say ...*You mean you don't know,* he divulged, "They don't want us to know about the men from outer space."

Now it was Spokes' turn to repeat: "The men from outer space?"

With all the patience of a grade school teacher, Chance attempted to explain how Andy Kaufman had been kidnapped by men from outer space. They'd been watching episodes of "Taxi" on their satellite dishes, and they were big fans of *Latka Gravis*—space people are smart, light years ahead of us—so they came and took him on tour.

Spokes didn't attempt to hide his incredulity: "Space people came and took Andy Kaufman on tour!" And if once wasn't enough, "Space people came and took Andy Kaufman on tour!"

"That's right!" Chance sounded relieved—like he was finally getting through.

A small troubled laugh broke to the surface as Spokes went on to ask, "And now he's back?"

"That's right! And we're going to start an act together."

"Are you going to do this new act here on earth? ...or in space?"

It was a perfectly good question, given the rest of the

250

conversation. Still, it didn't go over big with Chance. His face folded like a bad poker hand. He put his eyes on the table and furrowed his brow. He took to mumbling, something about having to call his agent, a jumble of incoherences, a reminder to himself—something about traveler's checks.

Spokes just sat and watched, and wondered. The city was full of people like Chance, deeply disturbed individuals slipping in and out of reality like a ghost through walls. He didn't know what to make of it. Guess it was just one of those cases of old friends who no longer have anything in common.

He paid for the pizza.

Chance was still rambling on unintelligibly as they stepped back out into the cold. He did, however, manage to tear himself away from the conversation with himself long enough to say goodbye. As Spokes wrapped his old friend in a parting hug, he pushed a roll of bills into the pocket of his threadbare overcoat.

It seemed early for the gathering dusk as Spokes moved off down the block, leaving Chance standing on the sidewalk. The wind had died down; the chill made the air feel stiff. Spokes didn't worry. Chance was a resourceful madman.

As Spokes turned the corner onto West Broadway, Clark and Olsen fell in step, one on each side.

"Where do you think you're going?" Clark was peeved. A punk kid like Spokes had given him, a veteran field agent, the slip.

Any answer would have been answering back. So why bother? Spokes threw him a bored look over his shoulder.

Clark wasn't waiting for an answer. "...And who was that dirtbag you were talking to? I've explained it to you over and over—we can't allow you to tell anyone that you work for us. That's classified information, mister."

"He's not anyone. In fact, he's not even himself."

"All the same, I'm going to have Olsen here pick that guy up and find out if he poses a breach of security." Clark glanced at his partner; Olsen registered the assignment with a barely perceptible nod.

Spokes stopped in his tracks, both palms coming up to make the gesture: *Now wait a minute!* "His name is Chance Langston. He's a friend of mine. ...Trust me on this one, you've got nothing to worry about. No one's going to believe anything he's got to say."

A dark Plymouth sedan pulled up to the curb. Clark went around to the other side. Olsen waited with Spokes by the curb. A second car, same model, pulled up and stopped one and a half car lengths back. Standard procedure. As Clark bent to get in behind the driver, Olsen's hand went for the door.

Spokes yawned, his hand flattening in front of his face to cover his mouth.

Olsen heard Clark's voice change his last directive: "Never mind about his dirtbag friend. The kid's right. No one'll believe him. Hang back. Sweep the route."

So Olsen went to take a seat in the backup vehicle. He had his instructions.

Spokes slid in next to Clark and smiled. It was a smile that made the FBI agent uncomfortable.